The Pirate Ship
and Other Stories

D1491830

Ruth Ainsworth

THE
PIRATE SHIP
and Other Stories

Illustrated by
SHIRLEY HUGHES

HEINEMANN : LONDON

William Heinemann Limited
10 Upper Grosvenor Street, London W1X 9PA

LONDON   MELBOURNE   TORONTO
JOHANNESBURG   AUCKLAND

434 92589 6

Set, printed and bound in Great Britain by
Fakenham Press Limited, Fakenham, Norfolk

Contents

Wake Up, Farmer Brown

The sun rose in the blue sky and shone down on the world beneath. The daisies opened and the birds in their nests began to chirp. The farm animals woke up too and stretched and yawned. They felt hungry.

Time passed, and though the animals heard the larks singing and the pigeons cooing, they did not hear the sound they were waiting for, the tramp, tramp, tramp of Farmer Brown's big boots coming across the yard to bring them their breakfast.

"Cock-a-doodle-doo!" crowed the cock. "Who will let us out of the hen-house and feed us?"

"Cluck! Cluck! Cluck! What can have happened?" said the hens, fluffing up their feathers to show they were upset.

"Moo! Moo! Moo!" said the cow. "Farmer Brown must come and milk me. I'm full of milk."

"Oink! Oink!" said the pigs. "Our trough is empty and so are our tummies. We do hope Farmer Brown

7

will come soon with our pail of delicious pig swill."

"Quack! Quack!" said the ducks. "Will no one let us out of the duck house? We ought to be out on the pond, looking for food among the waterweed."

"Meow! Meow!" said the cat. "I do want my milk. My saucer is quite dry and so am I."

"And I want my breakfast too," said the dog. "I've been awake for hours and hours and hours."

Then all the animals together called out loudly:

"Wake up, Farmer Brown and let us out and give us our breakfast."

But Farmer Brown didn't hear. His curtains stayed drawn. He went on sleeping.

"Please wake him up for us," said the animals to the sun.

"I'll try," said the sun, "if I can find a crack between the curtain, I'll wake him up."

The sun tried to find a crack and he found a little one and sent a golden sunbeam straight through. It landed on Farmer Brown's face. The sunbeam shone right on his eyes, glinting and gleaming. But Farmer Brown's eyes were tightly shut and he never felt anything.

"I found out one thing," said the sunbeam. "I looked at the clock that stands beside the bed and it had stopped. It wasn't ticking. It stopped in the middle of the night."

"Stopped!" said the animals. "He must have forgotten to wind it up."

"Of course the alarm never went off at six o'clock to wake Farmer Brown, as the clock had stopped," said the sunbeam.

"Then we must find some other way of waking him

up," said the animals, "or we shall never get any break-fast, or any dinner or supper either."

"I'll try to wake him," said the cat, "if I can get through the window."

So the cat climbed up the creeper on the wall and in through the open window. She landed softly on the bed. Farmer Brown never stirred. First she patted his cheek with a velvet paw.

Farmer Brown smiled in his sleep.

Then she tickled his nose with her whiskers.

Farmer Brown sneezed.

Then she bit an ear, very gently.

"Drat those flies!" murmured Farmer Brown.

Then she bit his ear a little harder.

Farmer Brown flicked at it with his finger.

Then she bit harder still, so her teeth left tiny marks.

Farmer Brown woke up and sat up and looked at the cat. Then he looked at the clock. He listened to it and found it wasn't ticking. He jumped out of bed and looked at his watch on the dressing-table.

"Eight o'clock

And not a penny got!" said Farmer Brown. "I'll be there in three shakes!" he shouted through the window and all the animals heard him.

One shake and he was dressed.

Two shakes and he was downstairs.

Three shakes and he was out in the yard. They all heard the tramp, tramp, tramp of his boots.

In next to no time, everyone had been let out and fed and the cow had been milked.

Then, and only then, Farmer Brown sat down in the

kitchen and had his own breakfast. How he enjoyed his porridge and bacon and toast. He was as hungry as his animals. He gave the cat an extra bowl of porridge and cream because it was she who had woken him in the end.

Straw For a Nest

Two sparrows wanted to build a nest and lay some eggs.

They wanted some twigs for the nest. They said to the oak tree: "Can you spare us some twigs? We want to build a nest and lay our eggs."

The oak tree said: "You can take what you like." So the sparrows took some twigs in their beaks and flew off.

Then the sparrows wanted some wool for their nest. They said to the sheep: "Can you spare us some wool? We want to build a nest and lay our eggs."

The sheep said: "You can take what you like." So the sparrows took some wool in their beaks and flew off.

Then the sparrows wanted some hairs for their nest. They said to the horse: "Can you spare us some hairs? We want to build a nest and lay our eggs."

The horse said: "You can take what you like." So the sparrows took some long, black hairs from his tail in their beaks and flew off.

Then the sparrows wanted some straw for their nest. They said to the hens: "Can you spare us some straw? We want to build a nest and lay our eggs."

The hens said: "No. We need all our straw for ourselves. It makes a soft place for us to lay our eggs."

The sparrows still wanted some straw for their nest. They said to the pet rabbit: "Can you spare us some straw? We want to build a nest and lay our eggs."

The pet rabbit said: "No. I need all my straw for

12

myself. It makes me a cosy bed for the night."

The sparrows still wanted some straw for their nest. They said to the strawberries: "Can you spare us some straw? We want to build a nest and lay our eggs."

The strawberries said: "No. We need all our straw for ourselves. It keeps our rosy faces off the dirty soil."

Then the sparrows were very sad because they could not build their nest without straw. They began to cry.

The scarecrow heard the sparrows crying and said: "Why are you sad?"

The sparrows said: "We are sad because we cannot get any straw and we cannot build our nest without straw. We have asked some hens, and a pet rabbit, and some strawberries. But they all said 'No'."

"I can help you," said the scarecrow. "My jacket is stuffed with straw. It is stuffed much too full. It tickles me. Please take what you like."

"Thank you," said the sparrows, and they took some straw in their beaks and flew off.

The sparrows built a very good nest with the twigs and the wool and the horse-hair and the straw. They laid five eggs in the nest.

The eggs hatched into five baby birds. When the baby birds could fly, their father and mother took them to visit the kind scarecrow, and to thank him for the straw.

The Little Wooden Soldier

There was once a little wooden soldier with a little wooden gun. He wanted to guard somebody, and keep them safe. But he lived in the back of a dark cupboard, and no one ever took him out.

So he made up his mind to go into the world and see what it was like. He started off one morning, tramp, tramp, tramp, in his black boots. Soon he came to a cat asleep in the sun.

"I'll guard this cat," said the little wooden soldier, and he marched up and down, taking care of the cat.

Then the cat woke up, and stretched.

"What are you doing," she asked, "marching up and down and waking me up?"

"I was guarding you," said the little wooden soldier.

"Well, I don't need guarding," said the cat. "Go away!" And she showed her sharp, pointed teeth, and her curved claws.

So the little wooden soldier went on his way, tramp, tramp, tramp, in his black boots. Soon he came to some baby chicks, pecking in the farmyard.

"I'll guard these baby chicks," said the little wooden soldier, and he marched around and around them, taking care of them.

Then the mother hen appeared, clucking loudly, and fluffing out her feathers. "Cluck! Cluck! Cluck! What are you doing to my baby chicks?"

"I was guarding them," said the little wooden soldier.

"Well, they don't need to be guarded," said the hen. "I can take care of them myself," and she snapped her beak in his face.

So the little wooden soldier went on his way, tramp, tramp, tramp, in his black boots. Soon he came to some baby ducklings. They were near the edge of a pond.

"I'll guard these ducklings," said the little wooden soldier. "I'll see that they don't fall into the pond," and he marched up and down, and was very busy keeping the ducklings safe.

Then the mother duck swam to shore, quacking loudly.

"What are you doing?" she asked. "Marching up and down so my children can't get into the water, which is their right place?"

"I was guarding them," said the little wooden soldier.

"Well, they don't need guarding, and they don't need to be kept away from the water. Come to me, children. Heads up! Paddle with your feet! That's the way!" and the ducklings swam along behind their mother, as happy as could be.

So the little wooden soldier went on his way, tramp, tramp, tramp, in his black boots. Soon he came to a snail, hiding under a leaf. Now a snail is a very, very timid person indeed, but the soldier thought he had better *ask* if she wanted to be guarded.

"I should like to be guarded very much," said the snail. "I never feel safe for a minute. I'm afraid of the thrush who is waiting to eat me. First he will crack my shell on a stone, and then he will gobble me up."

"Don't be afraid any more," said the little wooden soldier. "I'll watch out for that thrush and keep him away. You go where you please. I will take care of you."

So he followed the snail along the edge of the lawn, and across a flower bed, and under the rhubarb leaves. When the thrush came near, the little wooden soldier fired his gun, "Bang! Bang!" and the thrush flew away.

The little wooden soldier became quite well known in the garden. He guarded young caterpillars, and baby spiders, and families of beetles.

"Whatever did we do before we had a soldier of our own to take care of us?" said all the garden folk.

The Cock and the Hen

A Cock and a Hen once went into the wood to get nuts from the Hazel Tree. By mistake, the Cock let a nut fall and hit the Hen on the head. This hurt her very much and she began to cry. A man drove by and saw her crying. "Why do you cry?" he asked.

"Because the Cock hit me on the head with a nut," said the Hen.

The man drove on till he came to the Cock and called out to him:

"Little Cock, why did you throw a nut and hit the Hen right on her head?"

"Because the Hazel Tree tore my trousers," said the Cock.

So the man went on till he came to the Hazel Tree. Then he asked:

"Hazel Tree, why did you tear the Cock's trousers?"

"Because the Goats ate my bark," said the Hazel Tree.

So the man drove on till he came to the Goats. Then he asked:

"Goats, why did you eat the bark off the Hazel Tree?"

"Because the Goat-herd did not look after us," said the Goats.

So the man drove on till he came to the Goat-herd.
Then he asked:

"Goat-herd, why did you not look after the Goats?"

"Because the Farmer's Wife did not give me any
pancakes," said the Goat-herd.

18

So the man drove on till he came to the Farmer's Wife. Then he asked:

"Farmer's Wife, why didn't you give the Goat-herd any pancakes?"

"Because the Pig spilled my batter," said the Farmer's Wife.

So the man drove on till he came to the Pig. Then he asked:

"Pig, why did you spill the batter?"

"Because the Wolf carried off my Piglet," said the Pig.

So the man drove on till he came to the Wolf. Then he asked:

"Wolf, why did you carry off the little Piglet?"

"Because I was HUNGRY!" said the Wolf.

The Wolf showed his long teeth and his red tongue and the man thought he might *still* be hungry, so he drove away as fast as he could.

Russian Folk Tale

The Sunflower

A little brown sunflower seed lay buried in the soil. She heard the rain falling and felt the warmth of the sun, but she could not see the rain or the sunbeams. She was in the dark.

"I want to grow," said the little brown seed. "I want to grow and see the world for myself."

So she grew and she grew and she grew, and soon she pushed a green shoot out of the soil, and then two little green leaves like little green hands. It was lovely to feel the drops of rain on her hands and feel the sunshine warming her through and through.

She found she was growing beside a red brick wall. She grew as tall as one brick—then as two—then as three—and she went on growing till she was as tall as ten bricks. But still the top of the wall looked a long way off.

"I'll grow till I can look over the top of the wall," she said.

"Why not?" said the sun. "I'll warm you."

"Why not?" said the rain. "I'll see you're not thirsty."

"Why not?" said the wind. "I'll blow on you gently."

"Why not?" said the dew. "I'll freshen you."

"Why not?" said the soil. "I'll feed you."

So helped by the sun and the rain and the wind and the dew and the soil, she grew taller than all the other plants in the garden. Taller than the Canterbury bells and the foxgloves and the hollyhocks.

At last she could see over the wall. She now had a big, flat flower at the top of her stalk, with a dark centre and a ring of yellow petals all round like the sun and its rays.

Some children lived in the garden on the other side of the wall and they kept running down the path to look at her. They called their father and their mother and their friends to come as well.

21

"Isn't the sunflower beautiful?" they cried. "She's taller than we are and taller than our father and mother and taller than the high brick wall. Perhaps she's the tallest sunflower in the world."

"Perhaps I am," thought the sunflower. "Who knows?" and she smiled her golden smile at the children.

The children's father took a photograph of her and it was a coloured one that showed her yellow petals and her green leaves.

When the autumn came, the sunflower's petals began to fade and her leaves began to wither. She wondered what was happening to her and she was afraid. But the old gardener came by, with his wrinkled brown face and his dusty boots.

"Don't be frightened, sunflower," he said. "I shall collect all the seeds you have made when they are ripe and next year I shall plant them in a row beside the wall. Then they can grow tall and strong like you and look right over the wall into the next garden."

The sunflower was glad that she was going to have so many tall, golden-haired children and she let the gardener gather the seeds she had made, ready for next year.

"I'm ready for a long rest," she said, "after my busy summer. A long, quiet rest."

The Box Under the Table

Two kittens lived with their mother in a box under the kitchen table. One was called Pansy because her face was like a black, crumpled pansy. She was a good little kitten. The other was called Tip because he had a white tip to his tail. He was a bad little kitten. Their mother, Minnie, loved them both and thought they were the best kittens in the world.

The kitchen belonged to a woman in a white apron called Mrs Plum. She swept and dusted and poked the fire and rattled the pots and pans. Sometimes she filled a pail with soapy water and scrubbed the floor. When this happened, she lifted up the box with the kittens inside and put it on the kitchen table, so it should not get wet. Then the kittens had a good view of the whole kitchen, the dresser with the cups and saucers in neat rows, the clock on the mantelpiece, the shining brass door-handle, everything.

"How big the world is," said Tip, peeping over the edge of the box while Mrs Plum scrubbed the floor. "One day I shall explore every corner. Will you come with me?"

"I don't know," said little Pansy. "I am afraid of the monster with red tongues who lives inside the kitchen stove and eats lumps of coal. He roars and crackles."

"*I* am not afraid of him," said Tip bravely. "I shall go

right up to him and spit, like this -P-t-t! P-t-t! Then *he* will be afraid of *me*. I shall growl, too, like this -G-r-r! G-r-r!"

That morning, after the floor was dry, Mrs Plum put some milk into a saucer and lifted the kittens out of the box and stood them on the floor, one each side of the saucer. "You must learn to drink milk like your mother," said Mrs Plum. "Minnie! Minnie! Come and show your children how to lap milk."

Minnie came out from the brush cupboard where she had been watching a mouse-hole and her green eyes shone when she saw the milk. She stretched her neck till her mouth was level with the saucer and her pink tongue flicked in and out, flick-flick-flick and she lapped the milk. "Now, my kittens, you try to lap," she said. "It is quite easy."

Tip put his nose in too far and sneezed, A-tish-oo! A-tish-oo! and spluttered milk over the clean floor, but Minnie quickly licked it up before Mrs Plum noticed. Pansy got on a little better. She curved her tiny tongue and tried to flick it in and out and lap up the milk.

"You are very slow," said Minnie. "Now I am going into the garden to sharpen my claws on the apple tree. When I come in I hope the saucer will be empty. One day, when you can drink milk properly, I will take you into the garden and show you many wonderful things."

Minnie padded softly out of the kitchen.

"I don't like this horrid cold milk," said Tip. "Do you?"

"Not very much," sighed Pansy, "and I am tired of trying to lap."

24

"Let's paddle in the milk," said naughty Tip and he stood right in the middle of the saucer. When he got out, each paw left a milky mark like a star on the floor. Pansy paddled next and then her paws left milky stars as well. They pattered all over the floor leaving milky footprints everywhere.

Tip stopped by the coal scuttle and looked inside. "I shall try some of this coal," he said. "The fire-monster eats lots of it every day, so it should be nice." He licked a black lump till his tongue was as black as the coal.

"Is it good?" asked Pansy.

"It tastes very odd," said Tip, licking away. "Perhaps I shall be able to crackle and roar when I have eaten enough."

Just then they heard creak-creak-creak and thud-

thud-thud. This was Mrs Plum coming downstairs. The kittens scampered across the floor and scrambled into their box.

"What a mess!" said Mrs Plum looking at the milky footmarks. "I'll give you what-for."

The kittens did not know what "what-for" meant, but it sounded like something horrid, so they shut their eyes and pretended to be asleep.

When Minnie came in from the garden she was shocked to see the mess her kittens had made.

"It is no good snoring," she said crossly. "I know you are only pretending to be asleep. Now wake up and let me wash you properly." She started on Pansy and washed her from the tip of her pansy nose to the tip of her tail. Then came Tip's turn. He wriggled and squiggled and squeaked, but it was no good. Minnie held him firmly down with one paw and washed his ears and between his dusty little toes and everywhere.

"Tomorrow you must have another try with a saucer of milk," said Minnie. "Don't you want to grow into cats and climb trees and catch mice and sharpen your claws on the apple tree?"

"Yes, we do," said Tip and Pansy.

"Mother, tell me what 'what-for' is?" asked Tip. "Mrs Plum said she would give it to us if we were naughty."

"Well," said Minnie, "it might be a smack or it might be a shake. Or it might be both. I hope you will never find out."

The kittens hoped so too, and they made up their minds to be very good indeed.

The Magician's Boy

A magician lived in a lonely cave, making his spells and charms where no one would disturb him. But he was so busy, that he had no time to keep his cave tidy. He was always losing things and hunting for them in his drawers and cupboards and pockets. One day he mislaid his magic hat. The next day it was his magic wand. Another day it was his snakeskin gloves or his invisible slippers.

Worst of all, he used so many little bowls and basins and spoons when he was mixing spells that he never had time to wash them up. So he decided to have a boy to keep the place clean and tidy.

He soon found a boy, a simple farm lad who was in awe of the magician and thought himself lucky to work for such a remarkable person.

"All you have to do is to obey orders," said the magician. "Never touch anything without permission and never eat a crumb or drink a drop unless I give it to you. Terrible things have happened to boys who tasted some magic mixture."

The boy, whose name was Peterkin, did all he was told. If he got a smear of something on a finger he dared not even lick it off, for fear it might do him harm.

Sometimes he got tired of washing up all the fiddly bowls and basins which were first to be washed, then to be dried, and lastly stacked tidily on the shelf.

"Stir this mixture while I go out and get some nettles," said the magician one day. Peterkin took the bone spoon and began to stir busily. The mixture was pink and smelled delicious. The longer he stirred the more delicious it smelled.

"I don't think a tiny taste would do me any harm," thought Peterkin. "It might even do me good." So he ate a little off the end of the spoon. It tasted even better than it smelled. He supped a little more. I don't know how much he might have eaten but the magician came back with some nettles. Peterkin began to stir busily.

The next morning Peterkin had trouble while eating his breakfast. His teeth seemed specially sharp and twice he bit his tongue. Everything sounded so loud, too. The tick of the clock and the hiss of the boiling kettle almost deafened him. Suddenly he found his master staring at him.

"Peterkin, what have you been eating?" he shouted.

"Nothing," said Peterkin.

"Don't tell lies. You've eaten some of the magic mixture you were stirring yesterday. Look at yourself in the glass."

Peterkin got up and looked in the glass hanging on the wall. He saw that his ears were long and pointed and hairy and his teeth were yellow and enormous.

He burst into tears. "What's wrong?" he sobbed.

"Cheer up," said the magician. "You didn't eat enough to do much damage. You've only *begun* to change into a donkey—just the ears and teeth. Now if you'd eaten the lot, I might have found it very difficult to put you right."

The magician turned over the pages of his big book of spells and put a peacock's feather in the place as a marker. Then he shook various things up in a bottle, and poured out a dose.

"Drink this up, every drop."

Peterkin gulped it down and at once his teeth changed back to his small, even white ones and his ears became neat and pink.

Peterkin worked for the magician for many years and in the end he learned to be a magician himself, but he was always careful never to taste the magic mixtures he made. He didn't even lick the spoon.

The Scarecrow

A scarecrow stood all alone in the middle of a big, brown, ploughed field. The farmer made him to frighten away the crows from the corn.

The scarecrow had two sticks tied together to make his body and his arms and over these was a ragged coat and a pair of flapping trousers. His head was a turnip and on the turnip was a black hat. From the ends of one of the sticks, where his hands should have been, and round his neck, were strings threaded with bits of tinfoil. These jangled in a horrid way when the wind blew.

The crows believed he was a real man and dared not come very near, especially when they heard the rattle of the tinfoil. They flew about above the cornfield and cawed loudly, but they dared not come down on to the ground.

The scarecrow was very happy taking care of his field. He watched the clouds and sometimes an aeroplane flew by which was interesting. The sun warmed him and the rain did him no harm. His hat kept his head dry and his old coat was thick.

But there was one thing that he could not get used to and that was being all alone. There were no other scarecrows to talk to and not even a cow or a sheep with whom to have a chat. Occasionally the farm dog, Nell, came to visit him but she never stayed long.

"I must be off. I'm busy," she barked, and ran away towards the farmhouse.

One day, two little birds with red breasts flew across the field. They were not in the least frightened of the rattling tin-foil. They sat on his hat and chirruped together. Soon the cock bird said politely:

"Good morning, Mr Scarecrow. Our name is Robin. We should be much obliged if you would let us build a nest in your hat. There is a hole at one side that would make a fine front door."

"We have started several nests," went on Mrs Robin, "but we had to leave them all. First there was a hunting cat—then some boys kept interfering—and last time a greedy weasel began to visit us. It's getting late. I must lay my eggs soon."

"We should be so safe and comfortable here with you," went on Mr Robin.

"Of course you may build in my hat," said the scarecrow, smiling all over his turnip face. "It will be lovely to have some company."

Time flew by for the scarecrow. The robins collected dead leaves from the bottom of the hedge and moss and stalks for the nest, which they lined with sheep's wool and feathers. Then Mrs Robin laid her first egg, white with red speckles, and when she had laid six she sat on them to keep them warm. Mr Robin was kept busy feeding her.

The scarecrow quite forgot he had ever been lonely. He and Mrs Robin were company for each other and

Mr Robin often brought back tales of his adventures as well as a beakful of food for his wife.

This would have been enough for the scarecrow but there was another surprise in store. He felt a gentle scratching in one of his pockets and a mouse poked his head out and asked if he and his wife could make a nest in there.

"Of course you may," said the scarecrow. "The more the merrier!" and his life became even more exciting with baby robins in his hat and baby mice in his pocket.

Then, to complete his happiness, a timid hare made her form at his feet. This was only a hollow among the brown furrows but she brought up two little hares, as shy as their mother, but such clever little things. They could run almost as soon as they were born and always did exactly what they were told.

The scarecrow now had hardly any time to himself as he was always chatting to this animal or that, or doing some baby-sitting while the parents had an hour off duty. But he was never lonely and his turnip face was bright with smiles.

The Little Girl and the Bear

A little girl called Mary went into the forest to pick berries. When she had picked all she wanted, she looked for her friends and found they had gone home without her.

Now Mary was only a little girl and she could not find her way home alone. She wandered here and there till she was tired. Then she came to a little cottage and knocked on the door. But there was no one at home. She was so cold she went in and warmed herself by the blazing fire.

She had not been there long when a Big Brown Bear came in. It was his cottage and he lived there. He was very pleased to see Mary and he said:

"What is your name, my dear?"

"Mary," said Mary, who did not like the look of the bear. He was too big and his voice was too gruff.

"You can live here with me," said the Big Brown Bear. "I have been wanting a little girl like you to cook my meals and wash my clothes and keep the house clean. Now don't ever try to run away, because if you do I shall chase you and catch you and eat you up."

Mary did not like looking after the bear: but she did it, she had no choice. While she worked, she tried to think of a way to escape from the Big Brown Bear and get home. One day, she made a plan.

"Oh, Bear," she said. "Please will you take a present to my father and mother?"

"I will," said the Big Brown Bear.

Mary baked a big batch of tarts and she laid them in a great big basket and showed them to the bear.

"Don't you dare eat a single tart on the way," said Mary. "I shall climb up on to the roof so that I can watch you."

While the bear was getting ready, Mary crept into the basket and hid under the tarts. Then the Big Brown Bear took the basket on his back and set out. It was heavy with Mary inside it. Soon he sat down on a tree stump to rest and eat a tart, but Mary called out from the basket:

"I see you! I see you!"

"She can see a long way," thought the bear, and he went on again. Then he sat down on another tree stump and got ready to eat a tart, but again Mary called out:

"I see you! I see you!"

This happened every time he tried to have a rest and enjoy a tart.

When he got to the door of the cottage where Mary lived the dogs ran out and barked and snapped at him. He was so frightened that he put down the basket and ran for his life.

When Mary's father and mother opened the door and took in the basket and undid it, there was Mary, their little girl, laughing at them. They none of them ever saw the Big Brown Bear again.

Russian Folk Tale

The Squeaking Gate

There was once a gate who had a squeaky voice. The squeak was not unpleasant to hear and people in a hurry never noticed it. But people who opened the gate every day used to listen for it. It was a friendly little

voice that said: "Good morning," "good night," or "goodbye."

"Good morning," squeaked the gate to the postman and the newspaper boy and the milkman and the baker.

"Good morning, gate," said the postman and the newspaper boy and the milkman and the baker in return.

It made the gate feel important when these busy people spoke to him in such a friendly way.

Two children lived in the house and the gate was always glad when they ran down the path and never forgot to say "hullo" as they swung him open.

His favourite visitors were the cat and the dog because they were never in a hurry. The dog stood for hours looking through the bars and watching the traffic go by, and the cat even went to sleep on one of the gate posts. They always had time to chat.

Then, one unlucky day, the children's uncle came to stay. He was a very tidy man. He weeded the garden and swept up the leaves and when the gate ventured to say "good morning" in his squeaky voice, the uncle never bothered to say "good morning" back again. He looked very annoyed and swung the gate angrily to and fro and examined his hinges.

"I'll soon cure this frightful squeak," he said. "Just wait till I go and fetch the oil can."

Then he scraped the gate's hinges and dropped oil over them and he did the job so well that the poor gate had no voice left at all. He couldn't say a word.

"What's happened to you? Did you get out of bed the wrong side this morning?" asked the postman and the newspaper boy and the milkman and the baker. "Have you lost your tongue?"

The gate could not say a word in reply or explain that his voice had been all oiled away.

The cat and the dog were sad when they could not have any more nice chats, and the children got tired of saying "hullo" to a gate who never said "hullo" back.

The gate was miserable. He fretted and pined and became quite ill. His paint began to flake off. All the creatures in the garden were sorry for him but they did not know how to cheer him up.

One day, a family of mice came to live at the bottom of the laburnum tree that grew beside the gate. Their squeaky little voices reminded the gate of the days when he had had a squeaky voice of his own. His voice had begun to come back a little and when he could whisper, he whispered his sad story to the mice who listened to every word.

"We can help you," said the mice. "We'll call out greetings to your old friends when they open you. Would you like that?"

"Oh, yes, I would," whispered the gate.

So for some weeks the mice took it in turns to say "good morning" to the postman and the newspaper boy and the milkman and the baker, who were so pleased that they said a loud, cheerful "good morning" back again.

After a few weeks the gate's own voice came back. Perhaps the oil had got used up. He was able to speak to his friends and he specially enjoyed talking to the cat and the dog as he used to in the old days.

He was even happier now because he had the mice family to talk to as well. There were so many of them and their squeaky conversation was always full of news as mice have sharp ears and are very observant.

The Little Boy Who Did Not Want to Get Up

There was once a little boy lying asleep in bed. The sunbeams came in through the curtains and danced all over his face. But he didn't move. He just screwed up his eyes more tightly.

His mother came in to wake him. She drew back the curtains, and gave him a kiss, and said: "Time to get up!"

But the little boy only said:

> "I want to stay
> In bed all day;
> Please go away."

Then his father came in to wake him. He shook him and pulled back the bedclothes. But the little boy cuddled further down the bed, and said:

> "I want to stay
> In bed all day;
> Please go away."

Then his sister came in to wake him. She pulled his hair, quite hard, and told him to get up or he'd be late for school. But the little boy only said:

> "I want to stay
> In bed all day;
> Please go away."

Next the dog came. He stood on the rug beside the bed, and barked:

> "Bow-wow-wow!
> Get up now!"

But the little boy only said:

> "I want to stay
> In bed all day;
> Please go away."

Next the cat came. She sprang on to the bed, and licked his face with her rough tongue, and patted it with her paws, and mewed:

> "Me-ow! Me-ow!
> Get up now!"

and then she purred right into his ear, like a swarm of bees buzzing. But the little boy only said:

> "I want to stay
> In bed all day;
> Please go away."

There were many other noises outside that came through the window. The postman knocked. The milkman rattled his bottles. The coalman emptied sacks of coal, crash, crash. But the little boy never heard any of them. He was fast asleep.

Then something crept under the door and through the keyhole. It was the smell of bacon cooking. The little boy suddenly knew what was wrong. He was hungry! He was hungry as a hunter! He was hungry as ten hunters! He could almost hear the bacon crackling and sizzling in the pan.

The little boy was out of bed in a jiffy. He tore off his pyjamas. He dressed in two minutes. He was downstairs in three jumps. There were his father and his mother and his sister having breakfast. The dog was crunching his biscuits on the mat. The cat was drinking her milk out of her saucer. Soon the little boy was having *his* breakfast, too.

The Little Girl Who Did Not Want to Go to Bed

There was once a little girl who did not want to go to bed. When bedtime came, she said:

"I don't want to go to bed. I want to stay up and play."

So she crawled under the table and played with the
kitten. They played in and out of the legs of the chairs.
Then the kitten began to yawn and blink her eyes, and
soon she went off to the kitchen, and climbed into her
basket, and went to sleep.

So the little girl played on the stairs with the puppy
and his ball. Sometimes the ball rolled downstairs, and
sometimes it was the puppy, and sometimes it was the
little girl. Then the puppy began to yawn and blink his
eyes, and soon he went off to the kitchen, and jumped
into his box, and went to sleep.

So the little girl played with her two big sisters. They
played hide-and-seek all over the house. Then her two
sisters began to yawn and rub their eyes, and they went
upstairs to bed.

So the little girl asked her mother to tell her a story. It

was a long story, and when she got to the end her mother began to yawn and rub her eyes, and she went upstairs to bed.

So the little girl played a card game with her father, but at the end of the game her father began to yawn and rub his eyes, and he went upstairs to bed.

So there was only the little girl left awake in the house. Even the fire had gone out. She had a rock on the rocking-horse, but he was too sleepy to rock properly. She opened the dolls' house, but all the dolls were in bed. She looked for her teddy bear, but he was asleep too. She shook him to wake him up, but he just nodded off again.

So the little girl decided to go to bed after all. She took off her shoes and crept into bed with all her clothes on, because she was too sleepy to undress. She took her teddy bear into bed with her.

In the morning, when her mother came to wake her up, the little girl said to her:

"I needn't get dressed today because I *am* dressed. I went to bed with all my clothes on."

But her mother took one look at her, and laughed, and said:

"What nonsense! You look as if you've been pulled through a hedge backwards!" And she helped the little girl to take off her rumpled, crumpled clothes, and put on fresh, clean ones.

Water Baby

Once upon a time a Water Baby lived in a river. She was like an ordinary baby, but she could swim as well as a fish and she wore no clothes except a little green skirt made of water-weed.

Sometimes she played on the bank of the river or picked buttercups in the meadow. When she heard anyone coming, she dived back into the river, quick as a flash. If people saw the splash they just said to themselves: "Oh, that must have been a fish jumping."

The Water Baby had many friends. She liked the minnows who lived in the river. She liked the birds who whistled in the bushes. She liked the big black and white cows who ate the meadow grass. But sometimes she was a little lonely as there were no other Water Babies to play with.

One day, the postman came tramping across the meadow while the Water Baby was picking flowers. The Water Baby did not dive back into the river and hide because she knew the postman quite well. She often saw him crossing the meadow to go to the farm.

"Good morning, Water Baby," said the postman. "I have a letter for you. The children at the farm are giving a party and they are inviting every child in the village, so you can come too. Here is your invitation."

"Will you read it to me, please," said the Water Baby.

So the postman read it aloud:
"PLEASE WILL YOU COME TO OUR PARTY
TODAY AT WILLOW FARM."

"Can I go?" asked the Water Baby.

"Of course," said the postman. "You had better find
yourself some more clothes as you will look rather odd
dressed in water-weed. Of course you can go."

The Water Baby was very excited. She had never been to a party in her life. She had never played party games or eaten jellies or iced cakes. But wherever could she find some more clothes?

"Minnow," she asked. "How can I get some clothes to wear at the party?"

"I don't know," said the Minnow. "I've always had my neat, shiny scales. I never need any clothes."

So the Water Baby asked the Cow. "How can I get some clothes to wear at the party?"

"I don't know," said the Cow. "My coat just grows on me, in patches of black and white. I never need any clothes."

So the Water Baby asked the Bird in the Bush. "How can I get some clothes to wear at the party?"

"I don't know," said the Bird in the Bush. "These feathers grew all over me when I was in the nest with my mother. I never need any clothes."

The Water Baby felt sad because she could not find any clothes to wear like other children. She walked along the river bank, wondering what to do. Soon she came to a Scarecrow. The Scarecrow was just made of sticks, tied together by the farmer and dressed in some old clothes to make him look like a funny old man. He was supposed to frighten the birds away from the farmer's seeds.

"Scarecrow," said the Water Baby, "do you know how I can get some clothes to wear at the party?"

"You can have some of mine," said the Scarecrow. "I am far too hot in all these things the farmer put on me. What would you like?"

"Your coat is too big," said the Water Baby, "and

your hat is too big. Can I have your jersey?"

"Yes, certainly," said the Scarecrow. "I don't want it." He took off his coat and then he took off his jersey and gave it to the Water Baby. While he was putting on his coat again, the Water Baby tried to get into the jersey. She had a terrible time getting her arms into the sleeves. Then the kind Scarecrow did up the three buttons at the neck and the Water Baby was dressed for the party.

It was a lovely party. The Water Baby looked rather queer in her old, ragged jersey, but the other children did not mind. They did not laugh or stare. She had strawberries and cream for tea and a plate of jelly and she learned to play 'Here we go round the mulberry bush' and Musical Bumps.

When the party was over, Water Baby went back to the river. Her jersey tickled rather and she was glad to take it off and dive into the cool, clear water. It was nice to be a Water Baby again and she had a great deal to tell her friends, the minnows and the cows and the birds in the bushes.

The School Bus

Many children who live in the country have to go to school by bus. There was once a blue bus who had been doing this job for many years, taking the children to school in the next town. It was not difficult as there were no steep hills and not much traffic. Indeed, it was very pleasant when the sun was shining.

But the blue bus began to get tired of his daily drive. He got tired of stopping at exactly the same places at exactly the same times.

"I should like to go along different roads," he thought to himself, "and do just what I please. I'd like to go quickly if I felt like it, or to stand still and rest if I were hot."

The idea of doing just what he liked never left his mind. He dreamed about it at night and one day he decided he would make his dreams come true.

One bright, sunny morning, when he'd picked up the last of the children, he saw a tempting green field full of buttercups.

"That's where I'd like to be," he said to himself, "and that's where I'm going."

He turned off the smooth surface of the lane and began to go *bump—bump—bump* across the field. The children did not like this and some of the little ones began to cry. But the bus went slowly on, bumping his way through the long grass and the buttercups, till he came to the middle of the field. And there he stopped.

Almost at once all kinds of unpleasant and uncomfortable things began to happen. First, a cloud of black, buzzing flies began humming round his windows and, as some of the windows were open, they flew inside. Then the cows who had been peacefully eating grass came very close to him and began to lick him. One licked his headlights and made them smeary and another made scratches on his blue paint with her horns.

Then the bull who was among the cows came charging towards him with his head down, bellowing in a frightful way. The bus was so terrified that he shook with fear and his doors and windows rattled.

Even worse, all the children began to tease him and say:

"What a silly old bus you are! You don't know the way to school yet, after all this time. You ought to wear great big L plates so everyone could tell you aren't safe on the road."

The bus was beginning to think he'd better get back to the lane again when the farmer came into the field, from over a stile, red in the face and waving his stick.

"What's this?" he shouted. "What have we here? A poor old bus who's upsetting my cows so they'll give

no milk. You're not fit to be loose on the road. I shall report you to the police and I shouldn't be surprised if they sent you to the yard where old cars are broken up and sold for scrap."

The bus did not wait to hear any more. He started up and made for the lane and drove off as fast as he could towards the town. He left the cows and the angry farmer behind but some of the buzzing flies came too.

The children loved going so quickly and when they got out at the school gates a little boy patted his bonnet and whispered to him:

"Well done! We're not a minute late after all. We'll never never let you be broken up for scrap, never— never—never. You're a beautiful bus."

The blue bus never tried to leave the road again. He

went on being what he had been all his life, a steady, reliable school bus. He was resprayed to hide the scratches the cow had made on his paint and he looked (and felt) as good as new.

Kebeg

Once upon a time there was a little fairy calf no bigger than a pussy cat, with big, black eyes and a soft nose. He had a bell round his neck that rang ting-a-ling, ting-a-ling. He belonged to the fairies but sometimes he ran in the fields with the ordinary farm calves, although he was so tiny. His name was Kebeg.

One day, a farmer saw little Kebeg wandering in the meadows and he picked him up and put him in his pocket. "I'll take the little thing home for my little girl to play with," said the farmer.

When he got home and took Kebeg out of his pocket, his little girl, Jenny, was very pleased. She fed him with milk and kept him in an old rabbit hutch. Every day she took him for a walk, with a ribbon round his neck.

"Don't let go of the ribbon," said her mother. "Kebeg is a fairy calf and if you let go he will run back to the fairies."

"I don't think he'd ever run away from me," said Jenny, "because I love him so much."

One day, Jenny and Kebeg were out for a walk together. The little calf frisked and pranced, but Jenny kept tight hold of the end of the ribbon. Suddenly a little fairy man appeared, all dressed in green, with a pointed red hat.

"Would you like to come with me and see a fairy house?" said the Little Fellow.

"Yes, I would," said Jenny. "Has it a little chimney?"

"Yes, it has, with smoke coming out, too."

So they went off together, Jenny leading Kebeg by his ribbon. At last they came to a gorse bush. Under the gorse bush there was a dear little fairy house, no bigger than a turnip, with a thatched roof and smoke coming out of the chimney.

"Come inside," said the Little Fellow.

"I'm too big," said Jenny, "and the house is too small."

But as she watched, the house grew and grew till she could get inside the door. She was so excited that she let go the ribbon and Kebeg was left outside.

When evening came and Jenny had not come home, her father and mother went out to look for her. They thought they heard the faint sound of Kebeg's moo and they followed the sound, further and further, till they came to the gorse bush where Jenny had gone with the Little Fellow. There lay Jenny, fast asleep, and beside her was a burnt-out turnip lantern. The turnip was all that was left of the little fairy house.

Jenny's father carried her home, still asleep, and she never woke up till the next morning.

"Where is the fairy house?" she said when she woke. "And where is my Kebeg?"

She called his name day after day, and looked for him everywhere, but he was never seen again. The fairies were keeping him safe, this time. But she never forgot him, she loved him so much.

Manx Fairy Tale

54

The Sparrow Who Flew Too Far

A little sparrow lived in a nest in the ivy on an old stone wall. He had four brothers and sisters. When he had grown some soft brown feathers and could move his wings up and down, his mother began to teach him to fly.

"Stand on the edge of the nest," she said. "Then hold your head up and flap your wings and jump into the air. Then try to fly to the top of the wall. That will be far enough for the first day."

So the little sparrow stood on the edge of the nest. He held his head up and flapped his wings and jumped into the air. To his surprise, he did not fall—he found he could fly quite well.

I can fly farther than the top of the wall, he thought. I can fly over the field. Over the next hedge. Over the stream. I can see the wide world for myself. And he flapped his wings faster and faster.

At first he liked flying very much. Then his wings began to ache. And his head began to ache. And he knew he must stop and rest. He saw a nest at the top of an elm tree and he perched on the edge. It was a large, untidy nest, made of twigs.

"Please may I come inside and rest?" he asked.

A big black rook was sitting on the nest. "Can you say Caw! Caw! Caw!" said the big black rook.

"No. I can only say Cheep! Cheep! Cheep!"

"Then you must go away. You don't belong to my family."

He flew a little farther and he came to another nest, high in a holly tree. He perched on the edge.

"Please may I come inside and rest?" he asked.

A soft grey wood pigeon was sitting on the nest. "Can you say Coo! Coo! Coo!" said the soft grey wood pigeon.

"No. I can only say Cheep! Cheep! Cheep!"

"Then you must go away. You don't belong to my family."

He flew a little farther and he saw a hole in the trunk

of an oak tree. Surely he could creep in and rest his tired wings. He put his head in the hole.

"Please may I come inside and rest?" he asked.

A brown owl with a hooked beak lived in the hole. "Can you say Tu-whit! Tu-whoo!" said the brown owl.

"No. I can only say Cheep! Cheep! Cheep!"

"Then you must go away. You don't belong to my family."

He flew a little farther and he saw on the ground, by the edge of a pool, a nest of reeds and grasses. It looked so safe and comfortable. He hopped to the nest.

"Please may I come inside and rest?" he asked.

A wild duck with a flat yellow beak was sitting in the nest. "Can you say Quack! Quack! Quack!" said the wild duck.

"No. I can only say Cheep! Cheep! Cheep!"

"Then you must go away. You don't belong to my family."

It was getting dark and the little sparrow could not fly any more. He was much too tired. He just went hop, hop, hop, along the ground. Soon he saw another bird hopping along.

"Do I belong to you?" asked the tired little sparrow. "I can only say Cheep! Cheep! Cheep!"

"Of course you belong to me," said the other bird. "I am your mother and I have been looking for you all day. Perch on my back and I will carry you home."

So the little sparrow perched on his mother's back and she carried him home to the nest in the ivy and he fell asleep under her warm wings.

Go to Sleep, Charles

Charles had a bedroom all to himself. There was a picture on the wall of a little grey donkey galloping across a green field. The little donkey looked happy, kicking up his heels and waving his tail.

When Charles went to bed at night his mother tucked him up and kissed him, and he was asleep in a twinkling. When he opened his eyes it was morning once more. There was the little donkey, kicking up his heels and waving his tail, and the sun coming on to his bed, or perhaps the rain going pit-pat, pit-pat on the window.

One evening, Charles went to bed just as he always did. Mother tucked him up and kissed him, just as she always did. He snuggled down comfortably and closed his eyes—and then a very strange thing happened.

He didn't fall asleep! He turned on one side. Then he turned on the other. Then he lay on his back.

"Oh dear!" thought Charles. "I *am* tired of being awake."

After a long while his mother tip-toed into the room.

"Are you awake, Charles?" she asked.

"Yes," said Charles. "Wide awake."

"Are you too hot?"

"No, thank you."

"Or thirsty?"

"No, thank you."

"Or have you a pain?"

"No, thank you."

"Then I'll plump up your pillow," said Mother, "and you'll soon be asleep."

So she plumped up his pillow till it was cool and soft and cushiony, and Charles lay down again.

But he did not go to sleep. He heard an owl hooting as it flew among the trees. "Tu-whit, tu-whoo! Tu-whit, tu-whoo!" He heard his father playing the piano downstairs. He heard the cars go by in the lane. When his mother peeped in again he was still awake.

"I'll tell you a sleepy rhyme," said his mother. "Then you'll fall asleep."

"I don't think I shall," said Charles. "I'll never get to sleep. Never! Never! Never!"

"I think you will," said Mother. "It's a very, very sleepy rhyme. Shut your eyes."

So Charles lay still and shut his eyes and Mother began:

"Go to sleep, go to sleep,
    Into their holes the rabbits creep.
Hands fold, hands fold,
    Stars are staring with eyes of gold.
Lie still, lie still,
    Sheep are asleep on the grassy hill.
Feet rest, feet rest,
    Baby robins are in their nest.
Go to sleep, go to sleep,
    With rabbits and robins and curly sheep."

Charles gave a sleepy yawn and snuggled into his pillow, and Mother went on, saying the sleepy rhyme over and over again. When she finished saying it for the third time, Charles was fast asleep.

He never opened his eyes till it was morning and the sun was shining and the cock was crowing, "Cock-a-doodle-doo! Cock-a-doodle-doo!"

The Empty House

There was once a little boy called Hamish. He had a bear and a donkey and a dog and a Noah's Ark full of animals. But they were all stuffed with kapok or made of wood. They were toy animals. They didn't run about or make noises, except pretend ones.

"I want a live animal of my own," said Hamish. "First I'll make a house and then I'll go and look for something to come and live in it."

So he made a house with nails and a hammer and some wood. It had two rooms, a dark one for sleeping, and a light one for playing. He put straw in the dark one for a bed. Then he found a plate for food and a jar for water to put in the other one. He painted the house blue and then it was ready.

Hamish walked along the road and soon he met a duck. He said to the duck:

> "I've made a house
> And painted it blue,
> Please come and live there,
> I made it for you."

"Has it a pond near by where I can dibble and dabble?" asked the duck.

"No, it hasn't a pond," said Hamish sadly.

He walked a little further and he met a goose. He said to the goose:

"I've made a house
And painted it blue,
Please come and live there,
I made it for you."

"Is there plenty of long, green grass near by because I like eating grass?" asked the goose.

"No, there isn't any long green grass," said Hamish sadly.

He walked a little further and he met a pig with a curly tail. He said to the pig:

"I've made a house
And painted it blue,
Please come and live there,
I made it for you."

"Is there a lot of sticky black mud where I can rootle about?" asked the pig.

"No," said Hamish sadly. "There's no black mud where you can rootle about."

He walked a little further and he met a cat. He said to the cat:

"I've made a house
And painted it blue,
Please come and live there,
I made it for you."

"Has it a tree for me to climb and a hot fire where I can warm my back?" asked the cat.

"No," said Hamish sadly. "There isn't a tree and there isn't a fire."

He walked a little further and he met a dog. He said to the dog:

"I've made a house
  And painted it blue,
Please come and live there,
  I made it for you."

"Is there some soil where I can bury my bones?" asked the dog.

"No," said Hamish sadly. "There's no soil where you can bury your bones."

He walked a little further and he met a boy called Tim. He didn't ask him if he wanted the blue house to live in, but Tim spoke to him.

"What's wrong?" said Tim.

"I built a nice little house for someone to live in and no one wants to live there."

"Would it do for a rabbit?" asked Tim. "My pet rabbit is going to have some babies soon and I must find good homes for them."

"Yes, it would be just right for a rabbit," said Hamish.

When the rabbit babies were old enough to leave their mother, Hamish chose a sandy one with a white chest and he called it Jock. Jock loved his new house. He slept in the bedroom in the straw bed and he played in the other part. He ate carrots and lettuce from the plate and drank water from the jar.

Sometimes Tim came to tea and they had fun. They gave Jock a run on the lawn and then there were two of them to catch him when it was time for him to go back in his house.

The Queer Brown Stone

One morning, when the animals and birds woke up, they saw something strange in the middle of the lawn. It was hard and brown and rather round. It had no legs or arms or head or tail. Whatever could it be?

"I think it is just a queer brown stone," said the Robin. "I shall hop on top of it. It can be my hopping stone." And he hopped on top of it and fluttered his wings.

"I think it is a very large nut," said the Squirrel. "It is far too big to crack with my teeth. I shall try to think of some clever way of cracking the shell and getting at the nice part inside."

"I think it is a pie-dish, upside down," said the Kitten. "If I could turn it right way up, I could have my milk out of it." He tried to turn the queer thing over with his paw, but it was too heavy. He could not even lift the edge.

Just then, from one end of the queer thing, came a little flat head with two sharp black eyes. From the other end came a neat little tail. From the sides came four short, stumpy legs. The flat head snorted crossly: Snort! Snort! Snort! and an angry voice said:

"Am I a stone?"

"No," said the Robin, "you are not a stone. Stones can't talk."

"Am I a nut?"

"No," said the Squirrel, "you are not a nut. Nuts haven't legs."

"Am I a pie-dish turned upside down?"

"No," said the Kitten, "you are not a pie-dish turned upside down. Pie-dishes haven't heads and tails."

"I am a Tortoise," said the strange creature. "If I like this garden I shall stay and make my home here. I shall need lettuce and dandelion leaves to eat and a cosy corner where I can sleep."

"I will show you where the lettuces grow," said Robin, hopping slowly in front while Tortoise crept along behind. He led the way to the place where the tender young lettuces grew in tidy rows. Tortoise had a nice feast, with a nibble here and a nibble there.

"I will show you where the dandelions grow," said Squirrel, and he led Tortoise to a place where there were yellow dandelions and lots of rich green dandelion leaves. Tortoise ate all he wanted.

"I am tired now," said Tortoise, yawning and showing his pink tongue. "I should like a nice long rest."

"I will show you a cosy corner where you can sleep," said the Kitten and he took Tortoise to the rockery and found him a mossy bed among the ferns.

"Goodnight, Robin," said Tortoise. "Goodnight, Squirrel. Goodnight, Kitten. You have been so kind to me that I shall make my home in this garden."

He tucked his head away under his shell. He tucked his tail away and his four stumpy legs. Then he fell asleep.

The Car Who Wouldn't Go to Sleep

A little red car always spent the night in a big garage with heavy, sliding doors. There were a great many other cars in the garage with him. There were two small buses as well and a lorry and several vans. They all worked hard during the day and they were all glad to go quietly to sleep at night.

Sometimes one or other would relate an adventure he had had, perhaps an accident or being stopped by a police car, but usually a sleepy "Goodnight" was the most that was said.

But the little red car was never sleepy when it was time to settle for the night. He flashed his headlights and pooped his horn and fidgeted about. He moved a little way forward. Then a little way back. Then to one side. Then to the other. And all the time he talked in a loud, excited voice.

"Oh, I saw something so odd this morning. I met two elephants walking down the road. There were two little boys sitting on their backs. Do you think they were going to a zoo? Wasn't I lucky to see them?"

On and on he rattled, about this or that, and it was quite impossible for the other cars to get to sleep.

"Be quiet, can't you?" said the lorry. "I've been carrying sacks of wood all day and I'm tired out. I don't want to hear your silly chitter-chatter."

"Stop flashing your lights," said a bus. "If you'd carried as many passengers as I have and stopped and started as many times, you'd want to shut your eyes and rest."

"Don't fidget so," said the ice-cream van. "I must be fresh for my day's work or the children all over the town won't get their ice-creams. For goodness' sake put your brakes on and keep still."

When morning came and the garage man opened the big doors and it was time to start work, everyone was

tired and cross after their disturbed night. Some were difficult to start and others crashed their gears. That is, everyone except the little red car. He simply fell asleep. He always felt lively in the evening and sleepy in the morning.

The other cars complained to the garage man and said they would have to find another garage to sleep in because the little red car was so annoying and troublesome. They couldn't stand it any longer.

The garage man was worried and wondered what to do. At last he thought of a way out that might please everyone.

He sprayed the little red car a nice, glossy black and he gave him new number plates and a sign that said TAXI and lit up at night.

"You're not an ordinary car any longer," he said. "You're an all–night taxi. You can work all night while the other cars sleep, and you can sleep all day when the other cars are out working."

The little red car was delighted. He loved being an all-night taxi and whizzing through the dark streets with his lights on. He took people to railway stations and airports and to and from parties. Then, when it was morning, he was all ready to go quickly to sleep in the quiet garage.

So everyone was happy.

The Jack-in-the-Box

There was once a Jack-in-the-box. He was a very lively fellow and all the other toys liked him. His box was striped red and yellow and when the lid was lifted and he popped up, he was dressed in red and yellow too. He always had a smile on his face.

Inside Jack, under his clothes, was a strong metal spring and it was this that made him jump up so high.

One day, something went wrong. The lid of the box would not open, so Jack could not leap up. This made him very sad. He got bored and cross, shut up in the dark all day and every day. At night he used to cry and his crying kept the other toys awake. He could not sleep himself and they could not sleep either.

"We must do something to help poor Jack-in-the-box," said the other toys. "We must try to make his lid open again so that he can jump out and be happy as he used to be."

"I'll make the lid open," said the hammer from the tool set. "I'm strong. I'll give the lid such a bang that it will fly open."

The hammer had a red handle and a silver head and was very proud of his strength. He gave a great thump on the box, but the lid stayed shut.

"You've made my head ache," said Jack-in-the-box.

"I can do better than that," said the screwdriver. "I can get into cracks. I'll get under the lid and force it open."

The screwdriver got under the lid and began to force it open. The lid began to crack across the top, but it stayed shut.

"You nearly poked my eye out," grumbled the Jack-in-the-box.

"I'll give him a fright," said the donkey. "I'll creep up to him and then I'll bray loudly. He'll jump with surprise and his head will hit the lid and it will burst open."

The donkey crept quietly across the floor and when he got near the box he brayed his very loudest "hee-haw!"

But nothing happened. The Jack-in-the-box only complained that he was nearly deafened by the noise.

"I have a better plan," said the lion. "I'll roar and pretend I'm going to eat him up. He'll be so frightened and he'll try so hard to get away that he'll burst the box open. You wait and see."

The lion roared so fiercely that all the toys were scared. He sniffed at the box and growled.

"I'm coming to eat you up, Jack-in-the-box. Can you hear me grinding my teeth? You'll make a tasty supper."

"Don't be so stupid," said the Jack-in-the-box. "Even lions can't eat metal springs. Leave me alone."

Now there was a very old monkey who lived in a corner on the top shelf of the toy cupboard. His stuffing was coming out and he had lost an eye. Nobody took much notice of him. But he climbed down from the shelf and said:

"Let me try. I'm not as strong as the hammer or as fierce as the lion, but I've got proper hands and fingers.

And although I'm quiet, I do a great deal of thinking in my corner."

"You have only one eye," said the lion.

"But it's a very sharp one," said the monkey. Then, very quietly, with no bangs or thumps or roars, he felt the box with his clever fingers and he found a little catch at the side that kept the lid down. He unfastened the catch and the lid flew up and Jack jumped out, all smiles in his red and yellow coat.

"The catch had stuck," said the monkey. "It's all right now."

The catch never stuck again and Jack could jump up whenever he liked and he always had a special smile for the monkey on the top shelf.

The Dutch Doll

Once upon a time, there was a little girl called Jenny. Her uncle gave her a shining silver fifty-pence piece and she carried it about with her, tied in the corner of her handkerchief.

"Will you buy some sweets?" asked her father.

"Will you buy a book?" asked her mother.

But Jenny shook her head. She was going to buy something far better than sweets or a book. She was going to buy a Dutch Doll.

In the town where Jenny lived, there was a market every Saturday. The market people set up their stalls right in the middle of the main street. They sold fish and flowers and eggs and cabbages and many other things. Squeezed between the fish stall and the flower stall was a tiny little stall—really just a small table— where an old lady sold Dutch Dolls. There were dozens of Dutch Dolls, laid in rows and piled on top of each other. All made of wood. All costing exactly fifty pence.

When Saturday came, Jenny asked her mother to take her to the market, so she could choose her Dutch Doll. Mother held her hand and they made their way through crowds of women with their shopping baskets, till they came to the old lady with the Dutch Dolls.

The fish smelt very salt and fishy on one side and the flowers smelt very fresh and sweet on the other, but Jenny was too busy to notice. She was looking for her doll.

The Dutch Dolls had wooden heads and wooden bodies and wooden arms and wooden legs. The arms were jointed at the elbow, so they could move up and down. The legs were jointed at the knee, so they could move too. Each doll had black hair painted on her flat, wooden head, and black eyes and red lips. She had a dab of red on each cheek as well. And a sharp little wooden nose sticking out in the middle of her face.

"Hurry up and choose," said Mother. "They are all just the same. It does not matter which one you have."

But they did not look exactly the same to Jenny. Some had cheerful faces. Some looked cross. Some looked stupid. Some looked clever. It was very, very difficult to make up her mind.

"Hurry up," said Mother again. "I have a lot of shopping to do. Choose quickly and let's get on."

Jenny did not know which doll she liked best. One had specially red cheeks. Another had specially black hair. Then she noticed one that had a sad look on her face, as if she were lonely.

"I'll have *this* one, please," said Jenny, picking up the sad-faced doll. She untied the knot in the corner of her handkerchief and took out the fifty pence and gave it to the old lady.

"I shall call my Dutch Doll Greta," said Jenny, as they hurried through the market.

On the way home, they had to cross a bridge over the river. Jenny held Greta up, so she could see the river

75

below and the boats and the swans. But Greta still looked sad. Then, quite suddenly, Greta slipped right out of Jenny's hand and fell over the railing of the bridge, down, down, down, till she hit the water with a plop.

"Oh dear me!" cried Jenny. "She's gone. My poor, poor Greta. Whatever can I do?"

Then she heard another splash. A big, black dog, walking along the river-bank with his master, jumped into the water and swam towards Greta. As Greta was made of wood, she floated till the dog reached her and took her in his mouth and swam back to the bank.

Then he shook himself so that the drops showered all round, and laid Greta at his master's feet. He wagged his tail proudly and his master patted his wet head and said, "Good dog! Good dog!"

Jenny and her mother hurried over the bridge. "Thank you very much," said Jenny to the big black dog. "You saved Greta's life. And I was so fond of her because she is quite new."

The man was looking at Greta and said, "May I keep her till tomorrow and then bring her back? My dog's sharp teeth have scraped off some of her paint. I'll make her as good as new. Please tell me where you live."

"I live at Ivy Cottage," said Jenny.

"Then I'll bring her back early tomorrow."

Jenny missed Greta badly, but she made her a nice bed in a shoe-box and got some plasticine food ready; some red apples, some white eggs and some yellow buns.

The next morning the man with the dog rang the bell and handed Greta back to Jenny and Jenny thanked him and gave him a large, juicy bone for his dog's dinner.

When Jenny looked properly at Greta she said, "Why, her hair is blacker than ever! And her cheeks are redder than ever! And she has a SMILE on her face. A real, curly SMILE. She isn't sad any more. Falling in the river and being saved has cheered her up!"

The Car Who Never Grumbled

There was once a little old car who never grumbled. He lived in a shed that was old and shabby like himself. The shed needed a new coat of paint, and it needed a new door. There were holes in the roof that let the rain come in. But the old car never grumbled. He knew that *some* cars had to stay outside all day and all night. In summer their tyres were too hot when the sun shone on them. In winter they were covered with snow and the water froze in their radiators.

The little old car had been made a long time ago. He was fifty years old. There was a handle to fit in the bonnet which had to be swung before he could start. Even when he had started, he made a dreadful noise—clonk—clonk—clonk! Everyone could hear him coming and they had plenty of time to get out of his way.

The little old car had a horn to blow when he went round corners. It was made of rubber, and had to be squeezed. It said, "Poop! Poop!"

One sunny day, the little old car was chugging happily along. He was not in a hurry. He looked at the traffic going by. He waited for the traffic lights to turn green. He waited for the school children to cross the road. He waited for old people to cross the road.

Suddenly a big, fast car dashed by. The old car nearly fell into the ditch as the big fast one did not leave him

much room. But the old car liked the look of the big fast one which was pale blue, and long and low in shape. The old car knew it would start at the press of a button, and its horn was electric. It had big windows and two windscreen washers. It was very fine indeed.

Soon the big fast car came to a notice which said:

GO SLOW

Some men were mending the road and it was very rough. There were deep ruts and lots of sharp stones to go over. But the big fast car said: "That will not worry me! I have good tyres and good springs. I will just speed over the ruts and the sharp stones. I don't care!"

It bumped and bumped, and jolted up and down, and some luggage was thrown off its roof rack on to the ground. But the big fast car went on and on. It did not care. It did not even know it had lost some luggage.

When the little old car saw the notice which said:

he put on his brakes, and went very slowly. He knew his tyres and his springs were old. He crept over the deep ruts. He crept over the sharp stones. Then he saw, in the middle of the road, the luggage which had jolted off the roof of the big, fast car. There was a leather trunk on the ground, and a blue suitcase. The suitcase had burst open and there were dresses and slippers and a fur coat lying in the mud.

The little old car picked up all the luggage and put some of it in the boot, and the rest on the back seat. Then he drove off to the police station, clonk—clonk—clonk!

A policeman took the luggage into the police station and wrote everything down in his notebook. The number of the old car, and the date, and the time, and everything. He thanked the old car and swung the handle to start his engine again.

A few days later, a policeman called at the shed where the little old car lived, and knocked. He said that the fast, blue car was so pleased to get its luggage back safely, that it gave a reward of ten pounds to the old car for finding it, and taking it to the police station.

The old car was very pleased. "Whatever shall I do with ten pounds?" he thought. "Shall I mend the roof of my shed? Shall I paint my shed with green paint? Shall I buy myself a new seat cover?"

Then, all of a sudden, he thought of something much better.

"I will buy myself a fog lamp," he said. "That's what I'll do."

Now, when there is a fog, the little old car has a long, low, yellow beam of light, like a searchlight, coming from his fog lamp. It is so strong and useful that sometimes he can lead other cars home that are lost in the fog.

The Magic Bicycle

There was once a little girl called Dinah who had a red bicycle. It looked exactly like any other bicycle, with two wheels and a saddle and handlebars and a bell, but there was something very special about it. It was a magic bicycle.

If Dinah was quite alone with her bicycle she could get on it and say "upsa" and it rose up in the air and flew like an aeroplane, but it was much better than an aeroplane because it made no noise. It was quite silent.

When Dinah said "downsa" the bicycle came quickly and quietly down into the garden, or wherever she wanted to be. No one in the world except Dinah knew the magic words.

But a very inquisitive boy named Nick lived next door. He liked to spy on people, which is not a nice habit. One day, he crawled under the fence and hid behind a bush and watched Dinah playing with her bicycle. Dinah thought she was alone and she got on her bicycle and said "upsa" and at once they rose in the air and flew away over the house tops.

Nick could hardly believe his eyes and ears. He decided to get hold of the magic bicycle and say the magic word "upsa" and go flying through the air himself, without telling anybody.

So he waited till Dinah went out with her mother and then he got through the fence and got on to the red bicycle. His voice shook with excitement as he said "upsa" but the bicycle heard and understood, because it rose smoothly into the air and flew away over the roofs and chimney-pots.

At first, Nick enjoyed himself very much. He looked down on the houses and gardens and the traffic on the roads. He crossed over bridges and rivers and green parks where children were playing. Then the bicycle rose higher and flew faster. They left the houses behind and crossed some mountains and made for the open sea.

Nick got colder and colder and more and more frightened. Then he remembered that he didn't know the magic word which would bring the bicycle down to earth.

"Go back!" he shouted. "Go back, please! Turn round at once and go down! I want to go home! Turn back, please! Don't go any further! I don't like it!"

But the bicycle just flew on and on and took no notice. Perhaps it only understood magic words.

Nick began to cry. He cried so much that the tears

ran down his face and dripped off his chin on to the bicycle. He dared not leave go of the handlebars, even with one hand, to wipe them away. And he hadn't a handkerchief anyhow.

At last the bicycle said crossly:

"Do stop crying. Your salt tears will make me rusty and that would never do."

"I can't stop," sobbed Nick, "but I wish you would. Do, please, take me home."

"It seems a pity," said the bicycle. "I'm really enjoying myself and with luck we should reach land soon. I've always wanted to see Paris and the Eiffel Tower. But I can't risk getting rusty. I'm the only magic bicycle in the world."

"Please, please, take me home," begged Nick.

"Very well. But you must promise never to ride me again, and never to tell anyone that I'm magic."

"I promise," said Nick.

Then the bicycle turned round and sped swiftly home.

Nick kept half of his promise and never rode the bicycle again. But he didn't keep the other half. He told several of his friends that the bicycle was magic and could fly. His friends didn't believe him. They just laughed and said:

"Now who's telling stories? Do you expect us to believe such nonsense?"

The Pirate Ship

The good ship *Sea Lion* was a fine sight with her sails spread like wings to catch every breeze. Whatever the weather, her flag flew at the mast-head. It was the Jolly Roger, the pirate flag, with a skull and cross-bones on it. Any ship that saw this fearful flag made off as fast as possible in the opposite direction.

The pirate chief was Captain Bones. He had ten sailors in his crew, all with black sea-boots, and knives in their belts, and gold rings in their ears. They wore bright handkerchiefs tied round their heads, and they had frightening names like Pincher and Chopper and Scrag.

Life on board the *Sea Lion* was not very pleasant because there was no one to make the crew comfortable. They had to make their own beds and sew on their own buttons and do their own washing. The food was dull, too, as it nearly all came out of tins. They had bully-beef for dinner and supper on Sunday, Monday, Tuesday, Wednesday, Thursday and Saturday. The day that was different was Friday. On Friday they had fish which they caught fresh from the sea.

The pirates looked forward to Friday. They had the fun of catching the fish first and then the pleasure of eating it afterwards. Sometimes the cook fried chips as well, and then there was not a jollier pirate crew afloat, eating their fish and chips and passing the vinegar-bottle from hand to hand.

One Friday morning the crew settled down as usual to catch their fish for dinner. Some trailed nets behind the ship. Some had rods and lines. Some lowered little wicker cages over the side to catch lobsters and crabs. Only the cook was in his galley, polishing his pots and pans and slicing potatoes.

Time passed and no one had a single bite. The sun rose high and the deck became as hot as an oven, but still they had no luck. When it was almost dinner-time and the frying-pans shone like mirrors, there was still nothing to put in them. Then Captain Bones himself came on deck, carrying his own favourite fishing-net.

"I'll show you how to catch fish!" he roared. "Out of

my way and I'll show you how to set to work!'' He
threw his net over the side and waited a few minutes,
then began to haul it in. He hauled very slowly because
it was so heavy.

"I've a good catch here," he said, "enough for today
and tomorrow. It must be a shoal of herrings or else a
huge cod. It might even be a whale. Why, my net's
almost breaking! Lend a hand there! Look lively!''
Pincher and Chopper hurried forward to help, and
with a mighty heave they landed the net on deck.

"Shiver my timbers!" cried Captain Bones, when he
saw what he had caught.

"Here's a pretty kettle of fish!" exclaimed Pincher.

87

Chopper said nothing, but stared and stared with round eyes.

There, tangled in the net, was a plump, shining mermaid, complete with long, scaly tail. She had golden hair and held a harp in her hand.

The cook came up from the galley with his kitchen knife in his hand.

"Now I can start dinner," he said, "and about time too!"

"But—but you can't eat me," said the mermaid. "I am not a fish!"

"Begging your pardon, ma'am, you're half a fish. There are enough steaks in that tail of yours to give the crew a square meal and leave a nice bit over for fish-cakes."

The mermaid began to cry, her golden hair hanging over her face like a curtain and her tears dripping on to the deck. Even Captain Bones felt sorry for her.

"Well," he said at last. "If we don't eat you, what are we to have for dinner? We can't have bully-beef every day of the week. It's too much of a good thing."

The mermaid dried her eyes. "Let *me* cook your dinner today," she said. "Scrambled seagulls' eggs are very tasty."

"But we haven't any eggs—" began the cook.

"Never mind that. I'll see to the eggs."

The crew looked pleased at the thought of scrambled eggs, so the captain helped the mermaid out of the net and the cook took her down to his galley. She gave a shrill call through the port-hole and a line of seagulls, one behind the other, flew into the galley in turn and laid a large egg in the biggest basin. A few minutes

later, she and the cook were beating the eggs to a froth. Then they melted the butter and stirred up the scrambled eggs. The chips spat and sizzled, and when the bell went for dinner there was a piping hot meal on the table. The mermaid had even warmed the plates.

There was no talk of eating the mermaid after that. The captain gave her a cabin to herself, and in a few days she had settled down happily. She found some wool in a drawer and began to knit the captain a red pirate's cap with a tassel on top. When that was finished she started on stockings to wear inside his sea-boots. Her tail came in most useful for winding the wool.

In the evening, just as the sun was setting, the mermaid always seemed to feel lonely. She sat on deck, gazing out to sea, and playing sad tunes on her harp.

These sad tunes made the sailors think of their mothers and they wished they had never left home and run away to be bold, bad pirates.

But once the sun had set and it was time to make the cocoa for bedtime, the mermaid cheered up and the sailors cheered up too. They sipped their cocoa and told stories and asked riddles and wondered whatever they did before they had a mermaid on board, a mermaid with yellow hair and a silvery fish's tail.

One day, Captain Bones told the crew that he was going to marry the mermaid. "You must call her Mrs Bones in future," he ordered, "and do whatever she tells you."

The crew were upset by this news and they grumbled to each other as they did their work.

"Why should he have the mermaid all to himself?" complained Scrag. "She knits him caps and stockings, and I believe she has started on a jersey with yellow and black stripes."

"It isn't fair," agreed Pincher. "Have you seen the neat little shell buttons she has sewn on his shirt?"

"But we have to mend our own clothes," went on Chopper, "and do all the work of the ship!"

The next morning, when the captain went on his rounds to see that the crew were doing their duty, he was shocked to find that the deck had not been scrubbed. The brasses were not polished. The ropes were not tidily coiled.

"Look alive!" he roared. "This ship is a disgrace to any pirate. No work, no pay, you know."

Then Pincher, who was the bravest of the crew, came forward and made a speech:

"Captain Bones," he began, "we quite understand that this mermaid"—and here he bowed to Mrs Bones—"belongs to you because you caught her in your net, but we each want a mermaid of our own. When Mrs Bones plays her harp in the evening we feel lonely and sad. Please find us some more mermaids to comfort us, and then we will do our work and the ship will be spick and span from bow to stern. We'll work from morning until night."

Captain Bones looked worried. "It was a piece of good luck," he said, "my catching a mermaid. You can hardly expect me to catch ten more."

"I think I may be able to help," said Mrs Bones gently. "I have ten sisters who might care to leave their cave at the bottom of the sea and try life on board the *Sea Lion.*"

"Oh, thank you, thank you!" cried the happy pirates.

"You must try hard to make them feel at home," went on Mrs Bones. "The world under the water is very different from your world. It is cool and clean and quiet. My sisters are not used to loud voices or oily hands or rough ways."

The pirates promised to be very careful and they started straight away to prepare. They brushed their clothes and cut each other's hair and spring-cleaned the ship. Each made a present to give to his mermaid when she arrived. Pincher threaded a necklace of shells. Chopper carved a wooden spoon with a fish handle. Scrag made a dusting brush of seagulls' feathers. The others all thought of something suitable as well.

When all was ready, Mrs Bones called softly, and from among the waves rose ten golden heads, and then

ten white hands appeared, holding ten harps. The pirates let down rope ladders over the side of the ship and helped the mermaids to climb up on to the deck. Each mermaid was delighted with her present.

Life on board the *Sea Lion* was very different now that there were eleven ladies living there. The mermaids took it in turns to prepare the meals, and though their tastes were rather fishy, the men soon enjoyed their shrimp patties and lobster pies and seaweed salads. The deck was very crowded with mermaids knitting for their husbands, mermaids combing their hair and mermaids playing their harps. The pirates taught them to sing sea-songs and the mermaids taught the pirates some of their own under-water music. These are some of the songs they liked singing. Of course they sounded much better with the harps twanging, and the pirates' deep voices booming, and the mermaids' shrill voices fluting the high notes.

Every evening at sunset the same strange sadness came over the new mermaids as had come over the first one. They sat gazing over the waves, twanging their harps and sighing. Perhaps they wished they were little merbabies again, rocked in a cradle of coral with a pearl necklace round their necks and a little oyster-shell plate to eat off. But they soon cheered up.

The mermaids were very clean and tidy, and the ship was spotless. The only thing they did not like was the pirate flag, the Jolly Roger. "Such an ugly flag!" complained Mrs Bones. "Such a horrid subject to choose! My sisters and I will make a prettier one."

They each sewed part of the new flag, and when it was finished there were eleven different pictures worked on it. Every picture was something to do with the sea—a shell or a fish or a piece of seaweed. The pirates admired it very much. But of course they were not really pirates now, with no pirate flag flying and with eleven beautiful mermaids on board. They were sailors instead, which was much safer and better.

Before long, they reached a desert island. They went on shore to explore. The sailors left the deep footprints of their boots in the sand while the mermaids' tails made winding tracks behind them. The island had a spring of fresh water for drinking and palm trees with monkeys and parrots in the branches. They decided to live there for ever and ever and use the *Sea Lion* for fishing and for short trips round the coast.

The sailors built eleven palm-leaf huts and the mermaids set up housekeeping with half coconut shells for pudding basins. They lived happily ever after.

Cherry Pie

An old man and his wife lived together in a hut among the mountains. They were poor and hard working, but contented, and when they sat by the fire at night, the old man smoking his pipe and the old woman knitting, there was nothing in the wide world they wished for—except just one thing which they had given up hope of having, and that was a child of their own.

All the children who lived in the mountain village loved the old couple and on their way to school they would tap on the window of the hut and wave as they went by. On their way home, the old woman would sometimes beckon them in and give them a new, crisp biscuit, shaped like a shamrock leaf, or half a rosy apple. The old man was never too busy to mend the strap of a pair of skates or sew a buckle on a leather school bag.

At Christmas time, the old man and woman liked to give a present to every child in the village, from the babies to the big boys ready to go out into the world. They were so poor that they had to make the presents themselves. They made them of wool which they got from a relation who kept sheep down in the valley. The old woman spun the wool and the old man dyed it bright colours.

Together they made woolly balls for the babies,

94

mufflers and caps for the big children, and dolls for the ones in between. Even the little boys were pleased with a doll dressed like a shepherd or a sailor.

One Christmas, when the presents were all finished, the old woman set to work on something else. It was a big doll, as big as a real child.

"What are you doing?" asked the old man.

"I am making us a little boy," she replied.

His hair was made of dozens of loops of yellow wool and he had blue eyes and red cheeks. She dressed him in a red jersey and navy trousers and soft felt slippers. The old man made him a leather belt and a little wooden stool to sit on. As he sat on his stool by the fire, his legs in their navy trousers stretched out in front of him, he looked exactly as if he were alive, warming his feet in their neat grey slippers.

"If only he were really alive!" sighed the old woman. "If only he could speak and eat and play about! How happy I should be!"

On Christmas Eve they decided to take their child to the Wishing Well at midnight. The well was named the Well of Saint Nicholas and it was believed that anyone visiting it at midnight on Christmas Eve would have a wish granted. They wrapped the doll in a blanket and carried him to the well. It was a long, cold trudge, the snow sparkling with frost and the stars so large and bright that they seemed no higher than the church spire.

The well was frozen over and the old man broke the ice with a stone before they could dip their fingers in the freezing water and make the sign of the cross.

"Blessed Saint Nicholas, who loves the little ones,

grant life to the child we have made."

As they hurried home, their faces numb with cold, the old man thought he felt something stirring inside the blanket. When they were back in the hut, with the door shut, he set the doll down and at once he began capering round the room, dancing and jumping, stopping every now and then to hug and kiss his new father and mother.

The old people's joy was beyond words. They laughed and cried and kissed each other while the old woman prepared a bed beside their own. It was nearly morning before the child seemed tired and allowed himself to be put to bed by his new mother. He fell asleep at once, though his parents hardly closed their eyes as they got up so often to make sure he was still there, breathing gently, his yellow head half buried in the pillow.

Now life in the hut was very different. The child was always playing about and getting into mischief. He tangled his mother's knitting and hid his father's tobacco and spilt food on his red jersey. But his parents loved him far too much to be angry.

At first he could not speak, though he soon learned to understand what was said to him; then one day, at dinner, he said plainly: "Cherry pie," which was what he was eating. These were his first words and his parents called him Cherry Pie from that moment.

Cherry Pie loved the other children who came to marvel at him and he soon showed, by signs, that he wanted strong boots and a leather jacket such as they wore, so he could romp outside in the snow. His mother tried to keep him indoors where he was safe, but he pined and refused to eat and spent all day gazing out of the window. His rosy cheeks faded, and fearing that he would become ill, his parents gave him the boots and jacket he wanted, and a cap and gloves too, and he ran out into the snow to play with his friends.

Sliding, sledging, ski-ing, skating, Cherry Pie could do them all as well, or better, than the others and he soon learned to talk as fast as the others too. He begged to go to school and when he heard the school bell ringing he cried and sobbed till his father made him a school satchel and he went off every morning with his dinner inside, wrapped in a clean cloth.

97

Now Cherry Pie was a real boy. He could talk as well as everyone else and join in their games and learn his lessons.

"He's a real boy!" sighed his mother happily, as she darned a tear in his jersey.

"He's a real boy, a tough little fellow!" added his father proudly. "He can hold his own even with the bigger ones."

"He's just like us," said the other children when they went home after school. "He's just the same except that he doesn't feel hot or cold as we do, and if he pricks himself, sawdust comes out instead of blood."

But they were all wrong, the father and mother and the children. Cherry Pie was not just like the others. He was different. At first only the priest knew. His mother went to the priest to ask him to christen Cherry Pie and she was bitterly disappointed when he refused.

"Bring him to church—let him read the bible—let him sing hymns with his friends—but I do not feel I can christen him. I cannot be sure that he knows the difference between right and wrong."

"Indeed he does, Father," said Cherry Pie's mother. "If he has been up to mischief he hides when I come in. He knows he has been disobedient."

"Maybe! Maybe! But I'd like to wait before I receive him into the Holy Church. You're a good woman and you mustn't fret. Go on loving him and bringing him up carefully."

Sometimes the children at school and, indeed, everyone who knew Cherry Pie, were surprised at him. He would kick a kitten out of the way with his foot and when the other children said: "Don't do that. You'll hurt it!" Cherry Pie said, "All right," and he never did it again. Another day he would knock a smaller child over in a game and go on playing as if nothing had happened. When the others called out: "Look what you've done! Her knee is bleeding!" he would pick the child up and never be rough with her again. But that same day he might throw a boy's book into the stove and when his friends cried out: "How can he do his homework? What will he do without his book?" Cherry Pie would give the boy his own book, and would never again repeat that cruel trick.

Once he laughed to see a dead bird in the snow and Franz, his best friend, said to him: "Have a heart, Cherry Pie. Aren't you sad to see it cold and stiff?"

Cherry Pie ran home and asked his mother eagerly: "Have I a heart, mother?"

"No dear, you haven't," she replied.

"Why not? Why haven't I a heart like everyone else? Tell me why!"

"I suppose I forgot to make one for you."

"Then make one now, this minute?" For the first time Cherry Pie was in a rage and stamped his feet and shouted: "Make one now, before you cook the supper. I must have a heart."

His mother quietly looked out her work basket and some red flannel and made him a heart. He stood in silence, watching every stitch.

"Put it inside me, in the proper place," he ordered, when the heart was finished.

"But it might hurt you. I—I don't think I can do it. Please don't make me, Cherry Pie."

"You must do it," said Cherry Pie sternly. "You

must. If you don't I shall run away and never come back. I can't live here without a heart."

So his mother took out her scissors and her needle and thread and her thimble, and she put the heart inside him in its proper place, and sewed him up again. He never moved or spoke till she had finished. Then he jumped for joy and threw his arms round her neck.

"Mother," he said as he hugged her, "what is it I feel beating against me when you hold me close?"

"It is my heart beating."

Cherry Pie put his hand on his own chest and a puzzled look came over his face.

"My heart is still and quiet. It doesn't beat. Why doesn't it beat like yours?"

"I don't know, my little pigeon," said his mother

tenderly. "I cannot tell. I would do anything in the world to please you and so would your father, but we cannot make your heart beat."

Cherry Pie grew bigger like the other village children and did more difficult lessons at school and was more useful at home, helping to chop the wood and sweep the snow from the doorstep. Now and then he still hurt someone's feelings without knowing it, though he was sorry when it was explained to him. "I didn't know," he would say. "I never thought—It never occurred to me."

Kittens and puppies and very small children kept out of his way and hid when they saw him coming. He never knew why. He did not wish to harm them. Yet somehow he frightened them and upset them. He knew that he had a heart because he had seen his mother making it, but it did not seem to tell him what to do as it should.

One summer's day, Cherry Pie was walking by himself on the mountain side when he heard a sad bleating. Looking round, he saw a young kid that had somehow become separated from its mother. The little thing ran to him hopefully and began to suck his fingers and the sleeve of his jersey.

"Poor little thing, you're lost and hungry," said Cherry Pie. "I'll take you back to the herd and we'll soon find your mother. She'll feed you and comfort you."

He tried to coax the kid to follow him but the track was rough and stony and he found he had to carry it. Small though it was, it was heavier than he thought possible and he had to stop and rest many times before he reached the grassy alp where the goats were feeding. The kid ran bleating to its mother who was calling loudly for her lost child.

As Cherry Pie went back to the hut for his dinner, he felt a strange, warm glow. He even pushed up his sleeves and loosened the button at his collar. It was a new feeling, new and pleasant.

Another day, Cherry Pie was crouching behind a boulder, watching a chamois and her young one leaping from rock to rock. The mother went first and if the leap was very wide she waited for the young one, turning her head to encourage it and licking it when it was once again beside her. They were so beautiful that Cherry Pie could have watched all day. Their slender legs looked too fragile to bear them as they leapt and frolicked as if they had wings.

Suddenly he noticed that he was not alone. Two hunters were watching also. They held guns in their hands and had hunting knives hung at their belts. He could see the green tassels on their hats and the intent look on their faces.

Cherry Pie only knew the chamois were in danger and he ran forward, waving his arms and shouting. In a second the two animals were out of sight. He did not wait to hear the angry words of the huntsmen. He hurried home feeling, for the second time, a lovely glow of warmth.

"How rosy your cheeks are!" said his mother when he got back to the hut.

Some days later Cherry Pie was out for a walk with his friend Franz. Cherry Pie was wearing a pair of new boots his father had made. They had clusters of nails on the soles so he would not slip and the laces were tough leather thongs. The nails made patterns where the snow was soft. He felt proud as he strode along, proud of his stout, strong boots such as big boys wore.

The two boys climbed higher and higher above the village and nearer to the great glacier, the Sea of Glass, which was famous for many miles around.

"Shall we turn back?" said Franz. "I've never been as high as this without my father."

"Nor have I," said Cherry Pie, "but let's go on a little way. Let's go to the edge of the Sea of Glass and just set foot on it. Then we'll turn back."

"We haven't a rope," said Franz, "or an ice axe. Perhaps we should turn back now."

"Oh we're all right," said Cherry Pie. "My new boots won't slip. They can't slip, they're so well nailed."

"My boots aren't new," muttered Franz. "They're old and the nails are worn down."

"I'll hold your hand and then you'll feel safe," said Cherry Pie.

The Sea of Glass was so beautiful that the boys were glad they had come so far. It was blue and shone so brightly that they had to screw up their eyes. They tried a few steps on its polished surface, Cherry Pie going first, but almost at once Franz gave a cry of terror and there was a crackling, slithering sound. He had fallen down a crevasse, a deep crack in the ice.

Cherry Pie lay flat and peered over the edge. It was dark and horrible, but he could see Franz's blue cap far below.

"Are you all right, Franz?"

103

"Yes. I'm caught on a ledge but it's very narrow."

"Hold on. I'll let down my scarf and pull you up."

Cherry Pie unwound the long warm scarf his mother had knitted and lowered it down the crack.

"Can you reach the end, Franz?"

"No," came Franz's voice. "No. It isn't long enough."

Cherry Pie undid the leather belt his father had made and fixed it on to the scarf. He lowered this down the crevasse.

"Hold on, Franz."

The answer came more faintly. "I can't quite reach."

Cherry Pie thought quickly. What could he add to his home-made rope? A sock, perhaps? His jersey? Then he remembered his leather boot-laces. Fumbling in his hurry he undid one lace, then the other, and

knotted them on to the end. This time Franz's voice
said: "Yes. I've got it. I'm holding on."

"I'm going to pull you up," said Cherry Pie, but he
found that he was not strong enough. He could not
raise Franz an inch.

"You must hold on to your end and I'll hold on to
mine," said Cherry Pie. "Someone will pass by and
they will help. Just hold on."

Both boys held on, knowing that few people passed
that way, especially in winter. It was a lucky chance
that the priest went by, as dusk was gathering, having
visited a sick woman in the next village. He was able to
rescue Franz and carry him home. Cherry Pie stumbling along beside him. Stiff and numb though he was,
he felt the strange warmth spreading even to his icy
hands and feet.

When he lay in front of the fire, wrapped in blankets, his father and mother rubbing him and petting him, he suddenly cried out:

"My heart is beating! My heart is beating at last! Father! Mother! Feel it beating! That's why I felt warm even when I was lying on the ice."

Now the family in the hut had nothing else to wish for. They did not need to visit St Nicholas' Well again. The priest gladly christened Cherry Pie and from that time he never hurt anyone's feelings and the little children and animals ran to meet him, instead of hiding. His red flannel heart worked as well as everyone else's and told him what to do.

The Monkey Mouse

There was once a little boy whose name was George, but everyone called him Tiny. He was four years old, so you could not expect him to be very big. But he was rather small even for four. Some people thought he was only three and that was very annoying.

Tiny had two older sisters who had pigtails and played rounders and went to school. They could write in ink and one of them could knit. Their names were Judy and May. Judy was eight and May was seven.

People said to Tiny, "How nice for you to have two big sisters to look after you and play with you." Sometimes Tiny thought it was nice too, but sometimes he thought it was horrid.

When Judy and May read to him and played hide-and-seek with him, he was glad he had two sisters. When they said, "Go away!" or "You're too little to understand!" or things like that, he was sorry. When they whispered secrets to each other and did not let him hear, he cried with rage.

Judy had a pet white rabbit and May had a pair of brown guinea-pigs. They fed them and cleaned out their cages all by themselves. They went up the lane on their bicycles, looking for green stuff for their food.

Tiny wanted a pet as well. His mother had promised he could have one when he was old enough to take care of it properly. But Tiny wanted one *now*, this very minute.

One day Judy and May played at sending each other telegrams. One of them wrote a few words on a slip of yellow paper and stuck it up in an old envelope. They dressed Tiny up as a telegraph-boy. He had to ring the front door bell very loudly and knock with the knocker as well. Then he handed the telegram to whoever came to the door.

Tiny liked ringing the bell and banging the knocker, but he always wanted Judy or May to read the telegram aloud to him, and they wouldn't do this.

"You simply spoil the game," they said crossly. "Telegraph-boys never ask to hear what is in the telegrams. Don't be silly."

"Then I won't play," said Tiny. He stamped off with his hands behind him.

Tiny spent the rest of the morning being very busy. He knocked nails into an old wooden box. He turned out the rag-bag looking for some black cloth. He ran up and down stairs looking important. Judy and May wanted to know what he was doing.

"I shan't tell you," said Tiny.

"I will read you all the telegrams if you will tell us," said Judy.

"I shan't tell you," said Tiny again.

"I'll make you a paper boat," said May.

"I shan't tell you ever! Not if I live to be a hundred!" said Tiny. So the girls gave up asking. But they kept following him about and spying on him. He had to bolt the door of the playroom to keep them out.

In the afternoon Tiny went on with his secret. Judy felt a dab of sticky stuff on the door handle, so he must have been using glue. May found bits of fluff on the bathroom floor, so he must have been taking cotton-wool from the First Aid box.

There was more hammering to be heard. Then Tiny went for a walk and though the girls followed him through the laurels and among the raspberry canes, he gave them the slip and they lost him behind the hen-house.

At tea-time there were scratches on his legs and green paint on his fingers. Whatever had he been doing? They wanted to know so badly that they could hardly eat their tea. But Tiny was happy. He ate slice after slice of bread and honey. It was a wonder that he was not larger and fatter, he ate so much.

After tea Tiny went into his bedroom and locked the door, so no one could come in. Judy and May crept along the landing and laid their ears to the door and listened. Tiny was talking aloud. They heard him saying:

"How do you like your new house, my little one? Is the bed nice and soft? Have a drink of milk. Have a bite of supper. Would you like a nut or a bit of carrot? Here are some cake crumbs for your tea."

When their mother called Tiny for his drink of milk before his bath, they heard him say, "Goodbye, my dear little Monkey Mouse. I'll be back soon. Good-bye."

Tiny was careful to lock the door after him when he went downstairs. Judy and May went as well. While Tiny was drinking his milk, Judy asked, "What is a Monkey Mouse?"

Tiny looked surprised, but he replied quickly, "A Monkey Mouse is my new pet."

"What is he like?"

"He's like a Monkey Mouse, of course."

"Where did you find him?"

"In a place where Monkey Mice live."

"Does he bite? Is he fierce? Has he a name?"

Tiny wiped his milky mouth and said he had answered enough questions for one day. He went up to bed, singing a made-up song about "a Monkey Mouse in a nice, new house".

Judy ran to the bookcase and took out a book she had about animals. She looked in the index. She found the word MOUSE and the word MONKEY, but nowhere the words "Monkey Mouse" together.

May looked in another book called *Farm Animals* but it wasn't there either.

Then Judy looked in a large, fat, dull book with very small print that belonged to her father. Nearly all the words ever invented were in this book, but "Monkey Mouse" was not among them.

"I believe he made it all up," said Judy, slamming the large, fat book shut.

"So do I!" agreed May. "I don't know why we are taking any notice of him."

"I shan't bother any more."

"No. We'll just let him get on with his baby games."

The next morning, at breakfast, Tiny looked very pleased with himself.

"How's the Monkey Mouse?" asked father, from behind the newspaper.

"He's very well, thank you. Very well indeed."

"Do you want any bacon rind for him?" asked mother, as she stacked the plates.

"Yes, please. Bacon rind makes his fur shine."

Judy and May looked at each other. Supposing they were wrong after all? Supposing Tiny really and truly had a pet Monkey Mouse? They did not know what to think.

The Monkey Mouse seemed to need a good deal of care. Tiny was busy all day, off and on. He gathered clover leaves with the dew on them, for a cool salad. He mixed a drink of rose-petals and lavender which, he said, would make the Monkey Mouse well again if he ever felt ill.

The girls tried to play together and take no notice, but they felt they must follow Tiny and watch what he was doing. They asked questions all the time, dozens and dozens of questions. Sometimes Tiny answered them, and sometimes he said he was too busy. While he was threading some beads to make the Monkey Mouse a collar, Judy and May went to the summer-house to talk things over.

"Can you imagine a Monkey Mouse?" asked May.

"Not very well. We know it is small because it just fits into one hand."

"He says it has fur the colour of a brown egg."

"And eyes like yellow beads."

"And a tufty tail."

"It hums when it's happy."

"It spits when it's angry."

"It hates rice pudding and boiled milk."

"It likes peppermint creams."

"Tiny likes peppermint creams too," added May.

"And hates rice pudding and boiled milk," said Judy.

"He's just making it all up."

"Yes. I don't believe a word of it!"

Even though the girls agreed they did not believe a word, they went on watching Tiny and wondering.

That evening, when the three children were in bed, the girls decided to find out what the Monkey Mouse was really like. They planned to wait till Tiny was asleep and then to creep into his room and find out the truth, once and for all.

They waited till the clock in the hall struck nine.

Their parents were listening to the news on the wireless. Tiny must have been asleep for a long time as he went to bed at half-past six.

They tiptoed along the landing, Judy carrying the torch. Very, very slowly they opened Tiny's door. It creaked just a little. Very, very slowly they crossed the floor to Tiny's bed. The room was dark because the dark curtains were drawn.

Judy flashed her torch. On the chair by his bed was a square box, covered with a piece of black velvet. It was the Monkey Mouse's cage.

Judy shone her torch on to the chair. May swept off the black velvet. Underneath was a box with a door, painted green. May opened it and they looked inside.

There was a snug little cotton-wool nest in one corner. There was a doll's saucer with some food on it. There were a few twigs and leaves to play with. But no Monkey Mouse.

Judy put a finger in the bed and slowly drew it back. "The bed is warm," she whispered.

"And there's a very queer smell," added May.

"Look at the tiny tooth marks on that twig!"

"Are you sure the cage is empty?"

Judy shone her torch into every corner. There was nothing living there. Nothing at all.

Just then Tiny turned over and muttered something and flung out his arm. The girls tiptoed away so quickly that May never even put the velvet cloth back. Judy left the torch on the woolly rug where she had been kneeling.

They sprang into bed and went to sleep without another word.

113

Early the next morning, they were wakened by a shrill cry. Their father and mother woke up too. All four ran to Tiny's room. He was sitting up in bed with the tears running down his cheeks and gasping, between sobs.

"My Monkey Mouse is gone. My best Monkey Mouse. He can't bear light and that's why his house had to have a cover. Now someone has shone a torch on him and he's gone. I can see the torch on the floor."

"Perhaps he'll come back," said mother, drying his eyes.

"No he won't! He won't ever come back. He is very, very frightened of bright light. It blinds him."

Tiny was miserable all day. Judy and May were nearly as miserable themselves. They offered to read to him, to play hide-and-seek, to play telegrams, but he would not be comforted. He just wandered all over the house and garden like a lost child, calling his Monkey Mouse.

In the end Judy and May had to help him. They peered in cupboards and poked in corners. They shook the Wellington boots and the coats in the hall. They lay flat on carpets and reached their arms under things. Even mother looked behind her cake tins and under the gas cooker. But no one caught sight of a tuft of fur the colour of a brown egg. Tiny was crying so much that he could hardly see anything.

When father came home in the evening, he brought Tiny a goldfish in a bowl. It was such a lovely, lively goldfish, diving and swooping, and blowing round bubbles of air. Tiny simply had to cheer up. He gave the goldfish one pinch of special goldfish food and never stopped watching him till it was bedtime.

"Goldie is my own fish for always, isn't he?" he asked.

"Yes," said his father. "Your very own."

"And no one may feed him except me?"

"No one except you."

"And you'll show just me how to give him fresh water?"

"Yes. I'll show just you."

Tiny gave a sigh of happiness.

Judy and May were glad that Tiny had a special pet of

115

his own. Just before they went to sleep, Judy said, "Of course the Monkey Mouse was made up!"

"Of course!" agreed May.

"But the cotton-wool nest was warm. That wasn't made up."

"And the queer smell like the zoo was real."

"And Tiny's tears were real. He couldn't cry real tears for nothing."

"And something made the tiny tooth marks."

What do YOU think?

The Snow Bear

Once upon a time, two children lived among the mountains with their father and mother. Their names were Hans and Trudy. When they were very small indeed, they learned to walk safely up steep paths and over rough, slippery rocks.

Their father kept a flock of black goats which roamed over the mountain side, leaping over rock and crag on their thin, nimble legs.

The children's only playmate was a big dog, Leo, who helped their father with the goats. They had learned to walk when they were babies by pulling themselves up by his great shaggy ears and they had often ridden on his back as though he were a pony.

On their seventh birthday their mother bought them each a pair of climbing boots with nails in the soles and heels. Hans and Trudy were very proud of their boots. They liked the sound of the nails clinking on the rocks and they liked to be able to walk through wet, boggy places without getting their feet wet. Every birthday after that they had a new pair of boots as the old ones became too small.

The cottage where they lived was at the foot of a very high mountain called the Snow Bear. It was given this name because of a curiously shaped rock on the very top which, when covered with snow, looked like a huge white bear, sitting with his paws on his knees.

Sometimes, when their father took a day's holiday, the whole family packed up some food and climbed right up to the top of the mountain and ate their dinner at the foot of the Snow Bear who sheltered them from the icy cold wind.

One day, the children begged their parents to let them climb the mountain all by themselves.

"We know the way perfectly," pleaded Hans, "so we could not possibly get lost."

"We'll be very careful," went on Trudy, "and not leave the track or fall into a bog."

"Do please let us go!" they said both together.

"You are too young," replied their mother. "Wait till you are taller and stronger."

But their father was willing to let them go.

"What harm could come to them?" he said. "They are safe if they keep on the track and they have good, strong boots. It will do them good to be on their own. But mind what I say," he went on. "You must not linger on the summit by the Snow Bear. You must come straight down again. The sun sets early behind the mountains and once darkness falls you may miss the path. I wish you could take Leo," he added, "but I need him as three of the goats have strayed away."

The children promised not to linger on the top, so the very next day they got up early and put on their warm jerseys and their woollen caps and their thick red mittens and of course their beautiful nailed climbing boots. Their mother wrapped some food in a clean cloth and put it in a knapsack which Hans slung on his back.

"I will carry it up the mountain," he said, "and Trudy can carry it down."

Then they set off together up the steep track, often turning back to wave to their mother who stood at the cottage door, watching them. Then the path zigzagged and they could no longer see her white apron or the curl of smoke from the chimney.

At first all went well. The sun shone and the children felt so hot they took off their mittens and stuffed them in their pockets. Then Trudy kept lagging behind and Hans said impatiently: "What is wrong with you, Trudy? You can't be tired yet. We have hardly begun our climb."

"I'm not tired," said Trudy, "but something is pricking in my left boot. I must stop and see what is wrong."

So she sat down on a stone and unlaced her boot and took it off. She put her hand inside and sure enough, she felt a sharp metal point. It was the tip of one of the big nails which had worked its way through the sole and was hurting her foot.

"I will try to knock the nail down with a small stone," said Hans, looking round for a suitable one. But this was difficult to manage as the nail was near the toe and he could not get at it properly. They stood still, wondering what to do next. Just then they heard a curious tapping noise. Tap! Tap! Tap! A pause and then: Tap! Tap! Tap! again.

The children looked at each other in surprise. Who could be tapping on a lonely mountainside? Hans began exploring beside the path, among the bilberry bushes, and Trudy followed him. Presently they

119

almost tripped over a strange little man, no bigger than one of Trudy's dolls.

The strange little man was sitting cross-legged on a rock and beside him was a row of tiny hammers and pincers and other tools. There were nails as well and bits of leather. He was busy hammering at a bent nail, trying to straighten it.

He was dressed in ragged brown clothes and looked rather disagreeable. The same idea crossed the children's minds. If the little man were a cobbler, then he could do something about the pricking nail.

"Please, sir," said Trudy timidly. "Could you knock down a sharp nail in my boot?"

"I see you have some useful tools," went on Hans, gazing at the shining row. "It wouldn't take you long."

"I'm busy enough as it is," said the little man crossly. "But give me the boot."

Trudy set it on the rock beside him where it looked enormous. The little man could almost have got inside it. He soon saw what was wrong and with a pair of pincers he pulled out the troublesome nail. Then he chose the largest of his own nails and hammered it in in its place. The new nail did very well, though it was rather different from the others with a head shaped like a clover leaf.

"Thank you very much indeed," said Trudy, sitting down and putting on her boot. "It feels quite comfortable now."

"So it ought!" replied the little man with a scowl. "So it ought!"

"I'm sorry I've no money with me or I would pay for the nail," said Trudy, tying a double bow.

"What use would your money be to me?" snapped the little man. He looked such a thin, miserable creature that Hans said: "Perhaps you would accept something to eat? We have our dinner in this knapsack."

The little man seemed pleased and nodded his head. Hans unstrapped the knapsack and spread out the white cloth. Inside were two chunks of dry, black bread, two small pieces of cheese and two wrinkled yellow apples. This was all their mother could afford to give them.

"I hope he won't eat much," thought the children. "He is so small that he will only need a nibble." But they were mistaken. He seized a chunk of bread in both hands and began gobbling as if he were starving. The cheese went next, both pieces, and the rest of the bread. The children almost wept when he began on the apples.

121

Skin—pips—core—everything disappeared and only two stalks were left.

The little man tossed a few crumbs off the white cloth and folded it into a neat, flat square which Hans put back into the knapsack.

"A plain meal, but better than nothing," said the little man, shaking an apple pip out of his beard. "Now leave me in peace to get on with my work."

The children went on their way, the knapsack empty, and the sound of hammering started again from among the bilberries.

"What a greedy little man!" said Hans, who was already feeling hungry. "I never thought he would eat *all* our dinner."

"He must have been starving," said Trudy. "I wonder what he finds to eat and where he lives and how he gets clothes to fit him. I wish I knew. I did not like to ask him any questions for fear he flew into a rage."

"I've heard mother talk about little men of the mountains who occasionally appear to travellers. But she said they always brought good luck if you spoke to them politely. It wasn't good luck to lose our dinner, was it?"

"No," answered Trudy, "but it was good luck to have my boot put right."

They went on for some time in silence. The path became steeper and they had no breath to spare. When they looked down, the pine forest below was like green moss and the stream where their mother washed their clothes was only a silver thread. Some of the rocks were wet and slippery and they were glad the nails in their boots gave them a good grip. Suddenly, in the silence, they heard the sharp tap! tap! of the little man's hammer.

They both stood still. Where was he? How had he followed them so quickly? Was he hiding nearby to give them a fright? Then they noticed a patch of brilliant green in front of them.

"It may be a bog. I'll throw a stone in," said Hans, and he picked up a large stone and hurled it into the greenness. With a splash and then a horrid gurgle the stone was sucked under and only a few bubbles marked the spot.

Trudy took Hans by the hand. "Another step and *we* should have been sucked under like the stone," she said softly. "What a good thing we thought we heard the little man's hammer and stopped just in time."

They went on more carefully, looking out for patches of bog. The wind blew colder as they climbed higher and they put on their red mittens again. Soon, on a bare stretch of mountain side covered with great grey boulders, they heard the tap, tap of the hammer again, and stood still. Could the little man be hiding behind a boulder? But why had he followed them to such a bare, bleak spot?

Just then, from under a stone at their feet, glided a long, slender snake with yellow markings on his neck and his forked tongue ready to strike. He slid over the rough ground and under another rock and vanished.

"That was lucky for us," said Hans, sighing with relief. "If we had walked straight on we should have passed over the very rock where he was lying and he would have struck at our legs. His bite would have been poisonous."

"One of us might have died." Trudy shuddered.

"Yes. But we're both alive and well."

"The hammering has stopped," said Trudy. "I wonder where it came from."

They went on again and soon reached the last, steep stretch before the summit. They had to use both hands and scramble up as best they could. The wind blew colder still and their fingers were frozen even inside their mittens. When Hans was almost at the top and could see the Snow Bear rock plainly, he heard the tap! tap! of the hammer almost in his ear. He stopped a moment. What could be wrong now? Was there another deadly snake nearby with flickering forked tongue? Then he noticed that the rock just above him had some loose soil at the base. He grasped it lightly, not putting all his weight on it, but at once it rolled from its place and went crashing and thundering down the mountain side, loosening other rocks on its way. The noise echoed and echoed again.

Both children turned pale with horror. If Hans had put his weight on the rock and grasped it firmly then he, too, would have gone rolling down the mountain side, crashing to his death.

"We are so near now," said Trudy, "that nothing else can happen to us," and a few minutes later they were safe on the summit. Here the wind howled like a pack of wolves and chilled them to the very bone. They were thankful to get round to the other side of the Snow Bear and crouch down in the hollow between his great stone knees. Here was shelter and peace.

"If only we had our dinner," said Hans. "How good the bread would taste!"

"And the apples!" sighed Trudy. "I would even have eaten the core like the little man if I had had the chance."

"It is odd," remarked Hans, in a puzzled voice, "but my rucksack feels lumpy when I lean back on it. Could there possibly be anything left inside?"

"Take it off and make sure," advised Trudy, so Hans took it off his back and untied the cord that drew the mouth together and plunged his hand in. There was certainly *something* there, wrapped in the cloth. Hans quickly unrolled it and they could hardly believe their eyes when they saw what was inside.

First came two white loaves cut in thickly buttered slices. Then two creamy goat's milk cheeses. Last of all, two perfect rosy apples, their round cheeks shining like mirrors.

"I don't understand," marvelled Hans. "Mother never makes white bread."

"And the cream cheeses, who made them?"

"And no apples like these grow in our valley."

"Let's begin eating. However they got there, they are meant for us."

"Yes. You see the little man has brought us luck."

They ate very, very slowly and did not waste a crumb. The food was the best they had ever tasted. When they got up to start on the way down it was later than they thought. The sun was only just above the top of the nearby mountains and would soon set behind them. Then, as the children knew, darkness would follow.

"We must hurry," said Hans. "Come along, Trudy," and he began to scramble down the rough rocks.

126

"Wait for me!" begged Trudy. "I can't keep up if you go so fast and I'm so cold that my feet are numb."

"Quicker! Quicker!" urged Hans, slipping and sliding down the path. "If we're late home Mother will never let us go off on our own again."

The rim of the sun seemed to touch the nearest mountain top and then slip behind. Soon there was only half a sun showing. Then a quarter. Then no sun at all. Darkness fell and the children began to shiver with cold though they were hurrying as fast as they could, their woollen caps pulled down over their ears.

"Oh dear!" exclaimed Trudy, stumbling over a rock. "That must be the twentieth time I've bumped my knees or my elbows and now I've torn a great hole in my mitten. Why are you standing still, Hans?"

"Because I can't see the track," said Hans slowly. "Can you?"

Trudy peered down. There were just rocks and more rocks and still more rocks, large ones and small ones, jagged ones and smooth. There were no signs of any track.

"If we wait till the moon rises we shall be able to see the scratches our boots made coming up," said Hans. "Then we can follow them down. Let's sit in this sheltered corner and wait."

"It isn't very sheltered," said Trudy, as they huddled together under a large rock and listened to the wind howling round them. Trudy kept blowing into the hole in her torn mitten to try to warm her hand. Suddenly she cried out:

"Hans! Look! What are those tiny twinkling lights? Can't you see them, like sparks?"

"Yes, I see them," said Hans. "They make a winding trail all the way down the mountain side. I believe they are on the path. It winds just like that. Whatever can they be?"

"Let's follow them," suggested Trudy, "and not waste any more time. Come along."

The tiny, glowing sparks were a good guide and the children followed them easily, no longer frightened and no longer stumbling and hurting themselves.

"I've been thinking," said Trudy. "The little sparks shine every other step. It seems as though you or I must have made them on our way up, but how could we?"

"It might be——" began Hans and then stopped.

"Go on," said Trudy. "What might it be?"

"Well, it might be the nail the little man put in your boot, the special nail with the clover-shaped head."

"Why, of course!" agreed Trudy. "Of course you're right. It must be a magic nail. How kind of the little man to spare a magic one. Wherever it touched the ground coming up, there is a spark to guide us home. Mother was right about the little mountain men bringing good luck."

When they passed the place where they had last seen the little man among the bilberries, the sparks stopped. But this did not matter as they were nearly home and the path was wide and plain. They ran down the last gentle slope, helter-skelter, and saw their father outside the cottage door with a lantern in his hand. He was just coming out to look for them.

Their mother had set a lighted candle in every window so the little house was gay and welcoming. It was like a ship anchored in the darkness.

128

"You are late," said their father, while their mother hugged and kissed them and Leo licked their hands. "The sun set long ago."

"Don't scold us," pleaded Hans and Trudy. "When you hear the tale we have to tell you will understand and not be angry."

So they sat one each side of the fire on the wooden stools their father had made for them, and their mother gave them each a bowl brimming with bread and milk, steaming hot with brown sugar sprinkled on top. While they ate their supper they told the whole story. First the sharp nail and the little man of the mountains. Then the escape from the bog and the snake and the loose boulder. Then last of all, the lovely food inside the cloth and the trail of sparks leading safely home.

Their father and mother listened to every word.

"How very kind the little man was," said their mother. "I wish we could thank him ourselves."

"He did eat our dinner—every bit," said Hans.

"But he gave us a much grander one," added Trudy.

"We will give him some small gift and leave it among the bilberries where the children first saw him," said their father. "I have heard that the little men of the mountains are rich and have stores of gold and silver and jewels hidden in secret places underground. We need not choose anything rare and costly. Now we must go to bed because the children are tired and I have to be up at sunrise."

The next day, their mother got out her sewing basket and took an old mackintosh of Hans's from the drawer.

"I shall make the little man of the mountains a waterproof cape," she said. "You both noticed how

129

ragged and worn his clothes were. A cape will keep the poor little creature dry. Now give me your advice. How tall would he be?"

Hans and Trudy described his size as well as they could and their mother worked all the morning. By dinner-time the cape was finished. It had a button at the neck and two slits that his arms could poke through if necessary.

"Let's take it to the place at once," said the children, jumping up and down.

"Shall we hide and see if he comes to fetch it?" suggested Hans."

"Oh, no!" cried Trudy. "No! No! No! He would think we were spying on him and be dreadfully upset."

They ran up the mountain path and soon found the very spot among the bilberries where they had seen the little man. They knew it was the right place because they could see some marks on the stone where he had been hammering. They laid the cape near the marks and ran home to dinner.

The next day they visited the place again and the little cape had disappeared. The mist was falling like fine rain. How snug and dry he will be, they thought, in his little waterproof cape.

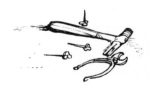

A Strange Christmas

Long ago, there was a good old man named Simon who lived on a small island in the middle of a large lake. He had had a long, useful life healing the sick and helping the poor, and now he was old he left the world and read and wrote and prayed. His white beard spread over his chest like mistletoe on an oak tree.

Simon was not entirely alone on his island. He had a little serving boy named Joseph who waited on him. Joseph's duty was to milk the goat, sweep out the huts with a broom made from twigs, and prepare the simple meals of goat's milk cheese and bannocks, which are flat oatcakes, varied by anything that happened to be in season, such as a handful of nuts, blackberries or mushrooms. He also grew potatoes in a little garden he had dug near by.

Simon lived in a hut of stones, roofed with branches, and smeared with mud to fill in the cracks. He had dried bracken for a bed, a rush mat, a table where he could work, a tree stump for a stool, and a chest where he kept his books.

Joseph lived in a smaller hut, with similar furniture. But while Simon's hut was neat and bare, Joseph's was full of all kinds of things to play with or to look at. He had made a ledge of stone and on this was a wonderful assortment of odds and ends. There were oak apples which he played with like marbles. A jar of water containing shining pebbles from the edge of the lake. A collection of feathers which he had picked up, speckled and flecked, and one of them, his favourite, bright blue. This came from a jay's wing. There was a whistle made from a hollow hemlock stem, a doll roughly carved from wood, and a bowl of wild flowers.

Once a month a boat came across the lake from the mainland and brought supplies for the next month, chiefly oatmeal for porridge and bannocks, and salt and a few dainties. The boatman sometimes brought his little girl with him and when this happened the two children played and romped together while Simon was writing his shopping list for the next visit.

Joseph's life was sometimes dull, but more often pleasant. He laughed and shouted as he climbed trees and swam in the lake, and he sang while he swept the floor or shook up the bracken beds. Sometimes he let the porridge burn or forgot to put salt in the bannocks, but Simon never scolded. When the wooden bowl of burnt porridge was brought to him he blessed it and said: "Thank you, my child," as if it had been properly made.

Although Simon and Joseph only spoke to another person once a month when the boat came, they made friends with the animals and birds who lived on the island or visited it.

One day Joseph found a curious round thing at the foot of a tree. It was like a ball made of twigs, strips of bark and moss woven together. He made a tiny hole by parting the weaving with his finger and inside he saw little, naked creatures huddled together.

132

"Master! Master!" he cried. "Come quickly!"

Simon closed his heavy book, first putting in a blade of grass for a marker, and came, leaning on his stick. But before he reached the scene Joseph had found out what the strange ball was. A pair of squirrels had come down from the tree and were crying pitifully, running anxiously to and fro, sniffing at the ball, looking up at Joseph, and then running up and down again.

"Is it their nest?" asked Joseph.

"Yes," replied Simon, "it is their drey. The young ones are inside. They are asking our help. See how heart-broken they are, and how afraid."

"I must put it back for them."

"Yes. Climb the tree and find a safe fork among the branches. Perhaps they will show you where it used to be."

As Joseph climbed the tree, carrying the drey carefully in one hand, the squirrels climbed faster and stopped at a point where three branches divided. Joseph lodged the drey among the branches as best he could and then the squirrels, with eager paws, wedged it safely into position.

Ever after that, the squirrels visited Simon and Joseph in the evening, bowing and bending their heads in gratitude, and rubbing against Simon's and Joseph's feet.

"They are grateful," said Simon. "They do not forget." And he caressed them with gentle fingers.

When Simon was reading or thinking he did not notice his surroundings. The goat might come into the hut and nibble any sheets of paper within reach, or the rain drive in through the open door, while Simon carried on with whatever he was doing. So it was small wonder that Joseph discovered a swallow's half-built nest where the wall and the roof met. Simon's cloak hung from a nail just there and the swallows had built a fold of the hood into their mud nest.

"Now see what has happened!" said Joseph. "Shall I free your cloak? The swallows can patch up their nest again. It's only half-made anyhow."

"I shall leave my cloak where it is till the swallows have finished their nest and laid their eggs and reared their young. They are our guests and we can grudge a guest nothing."

"But what will you do, how will you manage?" asked Joseph. "You've nothing else to wear when it rains or blows, and nothing else to spread over your feet at night. Supposing you get ill, I am too young to nurse you."

"We shall manage very well," said Simon. "I shall have to do without my cloak and that's an end of it. Don't be full of fear. Believe that all will be well."

So the swallows completed their nest like a mud cup, and laid their four freckled eggs, and four hungry beaky babies hatched out. Then the father and mother bird were busy from dawn till dusk, swooping after flies and carrying them to the gaping beaks which were never satisfied.

Their next visitor was a small one, and uninvited. One day, when Joseph took the lid off the oatmeal bin to make some of the flat bannocks which they ate daily, there was a little mouse struggling in the meal. The more frantically he struggled, the further he sank. His brown coat was powdered over with pale oatmeal.

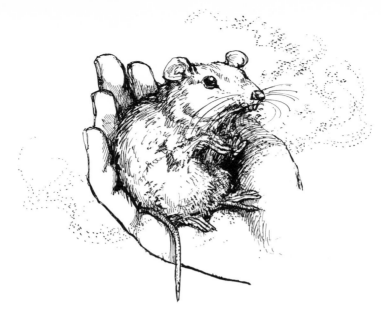

"A mouse is drowning in the meal bin!" called out Joseph.

Simon shut his book, not forgetting the grass marker, and came to see.

"Take him up gently," he said, "and blow him and brush him. He has had a terrible fright, but it is over."

Joseph held the little powdery creature in his hand and blew him until his fur was its original brown. Then the mouse sat up, no longer terrified, and cleared his eyes and his tiny ears with his paws.

"Go in peace," said Simon, "and keep out of harm's way."

The mouse turned his head briskly, looking from Simon's face to Joseph's, and then scampered off, stopping every few steps to look back.

"He might have been smothered," said Joseph, "if I hadn't gone to the bin just then."

The summer days went by and Joseph found so many things to do outside that he often neglected his duties. The broom stood unheeded in the corner, and the porridge was often too thick or too thin, and the bannocks over- or undercooked. He built a harbour of stones at the water's edge and made a fleet of twig boats with leaf sails. Some made cruises close to land, but every now and then he pointed one to the far mainland and launched it. As he launched it he sang:

"Go, little boat,
Keep afloat, keep afloat.
Go on your way
And return here some day."

For a long while he watched the tiny boat riding on the waves the wind had whipped up, over this crest, over the next and the next, till he lost sight of it. It became just a speck, just a fleck, on the shining lake.

On land he made a house for the wooden doll he had carved and named Samson. He pretended that Samson was strong and could do great deeds, such as build himself a house like a beehive, and dig a garden, and make a garden wall. Of course Joseph had to do these things himself but it was easy to imagine that Samson had done them.

One day, while playing on the far side of the island, Joseph came across a stag caught by his horns in some low branches. He had been running swiftly past the tree and had misjudged the distance. Both antlers were securely trapped.

His struggles had been frantic as the ground showed, with a bare patch worn and marked by the plunging hoofs. Now he was too weak to struggle and could

only turn his soft brown eyes and gaze at Joseph's face.

"Don't be frightened," said Joseph. "I can't get you free but I'll fetch my master and we will bring an axe and chop the branch down. Only a little longer and you'll be all right."

He put his cheek against the stag's soft one and tried to make him understand that he was coming back.

Simon and Joseph brought the axe and freed the stag who was too weak to run away. They led him to their hut and nursed him and fed him by hand till he was strong enough to toss his head and gallop off.

The autumn came and dead leaves floated in the lake. Blackberries ripened on the brambles and hazel nuts on the hazel tree. Then, just when the boat was due with its special cargo of things for Christmas, the great cold came.

Joseph had never felt such cold. He moved his bracken bed beside Simon's and they lay together under their blankets, with the old cloak over their feet. But the cold sank into their bones. Simon shivered and Joseph's teeth chattered. Even their hot porridge at breakfast did not warm them.

The lake froze and Joseph had to break a hole to get water. The wind blew from the north and found its way through the narrowest cracks between the stones of the wall. They were both too cold to work. They huddled over the fire with a blanket round them and told each other stories.

Then, one night, as they lit their evening candle, they saw the snow falling. In the morning the air was filled with whirling snowflakes.

They brought the goat into their hut and gave her a sup of porridge as well as themselves. Joseph fought his way to the shelter where the hay was stored and brought back as much as he could in his arms.

Then they began to get short of food. First they ate up all the potatoes. Then the few dried fruits they kept for treats, figs and dates. The oatmeal was getting low in the bin. Simon told Joseph to throw in three handfuls only for their porridge, one for each of them and one for the goat, and to make only six bannocks each day instead of twelve.

"The man with the boat will have to put on skates and skate to us," said Joseph, "pulling a sledge with all our provisions. But he could not find his way through this whirling snow. I wonder how thick it is on land?"

"It is a foot deep here on our island," said Simon, "and on the mainland there will be great drifts which

138

could swallow up a man and a sledge. We must wait and hope. Come, child, finish up my bannock. I have little appetite this morning."

The meal bin was now quite empty. A mouse could not have found enough for his supper. The goat munched his daily armfuls of hay and Joseph tried to munch a little with him. But it was too dry and harsh to swallow.

"I'll stew some," he said, and spent the morning boiling a handful of it in melted snow. But though he ate the mess that resulted, he was soon sick and felt emptier than ever.

It was necessary to have a fire, but impossible to find any sticks under the snow. Simon sadly, one by one, burned his books which were so precious to him, even the book with the capital letters illuminated in red and blue and gold. Tears rolled down his cheeks as he tore out page after page, and watched the gay pictures of flowers and birds and ferns go up in flames.

Joseph knew how hard it was for his master to burn his books, and he made up his mind that he, too, would make a sacrifice. He put his battered and beloved Samson on the fire. Samson burned well, with cheerful crackling and a red flame.

The goat, though she had her daily ration of hay, gave less and less milk. On Christmas Eve there was one cup each, a full one for Joseph, and half of one for Simon.

"What will happen to us?" said Joseph. "I'm frightened."

"Be calm," said Simon, putting his thin arm round the boy. "Wonderful things happen. The mouse in the meal bin did not know that you would save him. The squirrels thought their babies would perish. The stag was starving to death until we freed him. Let us believe that all will be well."

"But I can't believe. I'm too hungry to believe."

"Then I will believe for us both. Look, here are some sheets of paper that blew away. Add them to the fire."

Joseph did so and the flames leapt and crackled.

There was nothing, now, left to burn. The chest and table and stools had gone long ago.

"We will go to sleep," said Simon. "In the morning we will wish each other a happy Christmas."

Huddled under the blankets they felt the cold strike their bodies. But both old man and child fell into a peaceful sleep and forgot their troubles.

In the morning the sun was shining and the ice on the lake sparkled. The snow covering the trees and the huts was dazzling.

"A happy Christmas!" said Simon.

"A happy Christmas!" said Joseph. "And a happy Christmas to you, dear old nanny goat. But look! The goat has seen something! She is pointing with her horns and tossing her head."

The bright light was too strong for the old man's eyes, but Joseph screwed his up and peered over the ice.

"Look!" he said. "Look! Something dark is moving over the lake. A thin dark line, coming towards us."

The dark line came nearer. They could see that it was made up of tiny moving figures in single file. Then they saw what the moving figures were. They were hundreds and hundreds of mice, each with a sack on its back. The leader mouse ran up the side of the meal bin

140

and waited while Joseph took off the lid. Then it emptied its tiny sack and the ones following did the same. This went on till the bin was full.

Then, behind the mice, came a line of squirrels. They, too, carried sacks which they emptied into a heap in the corner of the hut. They contained hazel nuts which the squirrels had stored for the winter.

Hardly had the squirrels finished their task when the air was darkened by a flock of swallows, wheeling and darting round the hut. They had flown from the sunny land where they were spending the winter and in their beaks were twigs of ripe cherries, the twigs for the fire, and the cherries to eat. When they had finished there were twigs and to spare for fuel, and cherries enough for a feast. Then they circled round the hut before darting off towards the south where the sunny lands are.

"This is a real Christmas," said Joseph, throwing some dry sticks on the fire and sucking a cherry. "Shall we crack some nuts and then I'll make some bannocks."

"There is more to come, a fresh wonder," said Simon. "Look!"

Stepping delicately over the ice came a noble stag with others following. Each stag carried on his antlers, as on a reading desk, an open book.

Simon's hand trembled as he lifted off volume after volume, all the favourites he had burned and others that were new to him. The last of all was in large, clear writing with a picture on every page.

"It is a picture book for you," he said to Joseph, "and I will teach you to read the stories."

Then the stags bowed their heads and turned away, leaping lightly now that their burdens had been removed.

What a Christmas day it was, with the fire crackling and Simon and Joseph eating nuts and cherries, and a pile of twenty bannocks, perfectly baked, lying between them. Joseph had a reading lesson when they had eaten, and looked at the pictures in his book. He felt sure he would soon learn to read about the animals and ships and people in the pictures.

A week later the sledge came over the ice, drawn by the boatman on skates. They were glad of their stores and thankful, but nothing could give them as much pleasure as their unexpected Christmas presents, brought from so far by such strange messengers.

The Children With Green Hair

Once upon a time there were three sisters who lived in a wood. The eldest one was born when the red roses in her father's garden were in full bloom, so her parents named her Rose. She grew up with long dark hair, and lips and cheeks as red as a rose petal.

The second daughter was born when the snow was on the ground and only the pale snowdrops were flowering. So her parents named her Snowdrop. She grew up with pale golden hair like winter sunlight, and a skin as white as a snowdrop.

The third daughter was born when all the flowers in the garden seemed to be in bloom. Her parents did not know which name to choose for her. Then her mother said: "What is the sweet scent that blows in through the window?"

"It is the smell of the clover field beyond the wood," replied her husband. "The wind is blowing this way."

"Then let us call our new baby Clover," she suggested, and her husband agreed.

This third daughter grew up to be as pretty as pink and white clover, and as sweet as the scent of a clover field when the wind blows over it.

The little girls had few companions except each other, as the forest separated them from the nearest village, but they were not lonely. They played in the wood and when they were old enough they helped in the garden and the cottage, and took it in turns to carry their father's dinner to him, wrapped in a clean napkin. Their father was a wood-cutter and they could find where he was working by listening for the sound of his axe.

Sometimes he lit a great fire to clear away the stumps which he could not root up out of the ground. Then all three little girls, and their mother, would go to watch the fire and they sometimes baked potatoes or roasted apples in the hot ashes.

Clover was as happy as the day was long, but Rose

and Snowdrop were sometimes discontented. Rose would look at her red cheeks and lips, and thick black hair, in the shining brass tray that stood on the dresser, and she thought how pretty she was. She wished there were more people living nearby so they could admire her. She felt she was beautiful enough to marry a King and be his Queen.

Snowdrop, too, often looked at herself in the side of the copper kettle that her mother kept brightly polished. She gazed at her pale golden hair and white skin and wished that other people could see her and admire her. She felt she was lovely enough to marry a Prince and become his Princess.

Clover was too busy playing and running about to mind how she looked. She sometimes held up a spoon for fun, and saw herself reflected in the bowl of it, her face upside down and such a queer shape that it made her laugh. Then she opened her mouth to see her large white teeth, or pulled funny faces like a clown. She had no idea how pretty she really was, and there was no one to tell her.

The three girls were free to go wherever they liked in the wood, and to wander across the clover field, but there was one spot where they were forbidden to play. This spot was a deep, dark pool, with ferns growing round the edge, and great grey rocks sticking up out of the water like great stone animals bending down to drink. A rowan tree grew among these rocks and in the summer the bunches of rowan berries shone in the water like coral beads.

"Why can't we play by the pool?" begged Clover, "I want to sail boats on it, and gather some rowan berries

145

to thread for a necklace. I won't fall in. I'll be very careful."

"If you let Clover play there, then we want to go as well," pleaded Rose and Snowdrop. "We are older than she and stronger."

"You are none of you to go," said their father firmly. "It is no use begging and pleading because I shall never change my mind. There are queer stories about that pool. When I was a young lad, another boy went there with his fishing rod and he never came back to his home. They found his wicker fish basket on the bank, full of gold coins, but that didn't comfort his father or dry his mother's tears."

"But he was a boy," said Clover. "Boys do wild and dangerous things. Girls are more sensible."

"That's as it may be," her father went on. "But your grandmother told of a young lass who went to the pool one May morning to wash her hair, and she was never seen again. They found her sun bonnet tied to the rowan tree, full of pearls and rubies and diamonds, but that didn't help her poor parents."

When Rose's birthday came, and the garden was glowing with roses in bloom, Rose tied her hair with a new hair-ribbon that her mother had given her for a present. She peered at herself in the shining brass tray on the dresser, and turned her head this way and that to get a better view.

"I wish I could see myself properly," she complained. "Now, if I were to go to the pool, it would shine like a polished mirror in the sunshine and I could see myself clearly. I'll just slip out and have a look at myself, and nobody will be any the wiser."

So Rose left the cottage when no one was watching and ran through the wood towards the lonely, rocky place where the pool lay. She was out of breath when she reached the great grey rocks, lifting stony shoulders out of the water, and the solitary rowan tree bending its branches.

She knelt down and gazed into the dark, smooth surface. The new ribbon looked very bright in her black hair. As she gazed, ripples suddenly covered the water and up rose a tall, majestic figure with a crown on his head and a floating cloak of water-weed. There was a strange, greenish tinge about the person's hair and beard, but his voice was kind and firm.

"I am pleased to see you, Rose. I am the King of this pool and I have long hoped to meet you. I have heard of your beauty. Will you come back with me to my kingdom under the water, and serve me for a year? Then you may return to your father and mother and two sisters. I shall reward you suitably."

" How can I serve your majesty?" asked Rose. "I am only a simple girl."

"You can be a nurse for my children, the young princes and princesses. You shall wear fine clothes and priceless jewels, and I will give you a crystal mirror of your own. Please come!"

Rose liked the idea of the rich clothes and jewels. "It is only for a year," she thought to herself, "and I can always go home if I am unhappy. I know the way."

"Yes, I agree," she said, and the King took her warm hands in his cold ones and pulled her down, down, down into the depths of the dark pool.

Here she found herself in another world, very

different from the one she had come from. There were flowers, trees, meadows and roads, glowing as if lit by invisible lamps. The people living in this under-water kingdom glided here and there silently, leaving no footprints on the sandy ground.

The Queen was beautiful and gentle, and the royal children were lively as minnows. They had green hair and silver hands and feet, and were very mischievous. Rose was delighted with her new clothes, embroidered with jewels, and spent as much time as she could spare admiring herself in the crystal mirror.

"You may do whatever you think best with our children," said the King, "but you must on no account strike them. You may scold them if they are naughty, but never raise your hand to them."

At first all went well. If the royal children were troublesome Rose had only to tell them a story about her life in the cottage in the wood, and they would sit as quiet as shells, listening and asking for more. But one day, one of the little princes was chasing one of his sisters and he caught his silver foot in Rose's dress, and there was a tearing sound.

"You clumsy boy!" shouted Rose, "you've torn my beautiful dress!" and she gave him a slap. In a moment the King stood before her, taller and more majestic than ever.

"You must go now," he said sadly, "and never come back. Here are your wages." He handed her a heavy purse and in a twinkling she found herself on the shore of the pool, wearing her old cotton dress, and clutching the purse.

She ran home as fast as she could and found her

148

parents and her two sisters having tea together. They kissed her and hugged her, and her mother cried with joy because she had given up hope of seeing her eldest daughter again.

Rose told her story and at the end she remembered her reward and opened the purse. But it was filled with broken shells, not gold coins as she had expected. She began to stamp her feet and protest that it wasn't fair, but her father stopped her.

"Be silent, my daughter. The Water Folk treated you kindly and have allowed you to come home to us, safe and well. You broke *your* part of the bargain by striking the little prince. You cannot complain that the King has withheld whatever reward he had planned."

The days passed by and Rose often told her two sisters stories of her life with the King and the Queen and the royal children. She described the lovely clothes she wore and the jewels, and remembered only the times when the green-haired children were good and obedient, clapping their silver hands when she played with them, and dancing on their silver feet.

When the winter came and Snowdrop's birthday, her parents gave her a pair of ear-rings. She put them on and peered at herself in the polished side of the copper kettle. Like her sister Rose, she thought she could see herself much more plainly if she slipped away to the pool and had a quick look in its shining surface. No one need know.

She chose a moment when the rest of the family were occupied and ran off in the direction of the pool. The rowan tree was bare and swayed in the wind and the pool was crisped with ripples, but she found a smooth patch of water under one of the great rocks. As she bent over, her ear-rings gleamed in the pale wintry sunshine. Suddenly a wave broke against the rock and from the middle of the pool rose a tall, majestic figure with a crown on his head and a floating cloak of water-weed. She noticed a strange, greenish tinge about the person's hair and beard. She was not surprised when he spoke to her, and said:

"I am pleased to see you, Snowdrop. I am the King of this pool and I have long hoped to meet you. I have heard of your beauty. Will you come back with me to my kingdom under the water and serve me for a year? Then you may return to your father and mother and two sisters. I shall reward you suitably."

"What can I do to serve your majesty?" asked Snowdrop.

"You can be a nurse for my children, the young princes and princesses."

Snowdrop agreed, thinking, like Rose, that she could always go home if she were unhappy. The King took her warm hands in his cold ones and pulled her down, down, down into the depths of the dark pool.

Here she found herself in a different world, just as Rose had described. She was given fine clothes and jewels and a crystal mirror. She was kindly treated by the gentle Queen and soon learned the names of the little princes and princesses. She had to comb their green hair and see that they washed their silver hands.

"Do what you think best with the royal children," said the King, "but you must on no account strike them. You may scold them if they are naughty, but never raise your hand to them."

151

For some time all went well. Snowdrop was more patient than her sister Rose and the children grew to love her dearly. She taught them songs and games and when they were tiresome she had only to speak a sharp word and they would behave themselves.

But one day the eldest princess upset Snowdrop's jewel box and the contents scattered on to the sandy floor.

"You careless child! See what you have done!" scolded Snowdrop and she gave the girl a slap. At once the King appeared before her, tall and majestic.

"You must go now," he said sadly, "and never come back. Here are your wages." He handed her a heavy purse and in a twinkling she found herself on the shore of the pool, wearing her ordinary clothes.

Her family welcomed her home and she told them everything that had happened. When she opened the purse, she found it was stuffed with fish bones. She hung her head because she knew that she had not kept her part of the bargain.

The three girls kept far away from the pool till the season when the clover field was in full bloom. Then Rose said to Clover:

"Now it is your birthday, why don't you go to the pool and try your luck?"

"No, thank you," said Clover, laughing. "I like being here, at home."

"But don't you want to wear fine dresses and sparkling jewels?"

"No, I don't! And I don't want to come home with a purse of broken shells or fish bones, either!"

"Will you visit the pool for my sake?" begged Rose.

152

"I lost my hair ribbon when I was there. Perhaps you'll find it among the rushes."

"And I lost an ear-ring," added Snowdrop. "It may be lying on the rock where I knelt and leaned over. Do go and look for me."

"You can go yourselves," said Clover.

But her sisters protested that they dared not go. The King of the pool might be angry and would perhaps drive them away roughly, or even take them as prisoners to his watery kingdom.

"Very well," said Clover. "I'll walk round the pool just once and if I haven't found your ribbon or your ear-ring then, I shall come straight home. Goodbye."

Clover hurried off to the pool and when she got there she was glad she had agreed to come. The water shone brightly and the rowan berries were forming in green bunches which would later turn red as coral. The rocks, more than ever, looked like sleeping animals, sunbathing at the edge of the pool. There was not a sound to be heard and the wind scarcely stirred the rushes. As Clover watched, she forgot about the lost ribbon and ear-ring and thought only how peaceful it was in this wild and lonely place.

She started with surprise when the waters of the pool parted and the tall, majestic figure of the King appeared. He at once called her by her name and asked her to be a nurse to the little princes and princesses for a year.

"No, thank you, Your Majesty," said Clover. "My two older sisters did not please you and I am younger than they. I may not please you either."

"You are different from them," went on the King.

"You are kinder and more patient. You shall have all the fine clothes and jewels your heart can desire, and a crystal mirror to gaze in."

Clover laughed and answered: "I do not want fine dresses or jewels or a mirror. I like my own dress that my mother made for me best. I am not grand enough to live with a King and a Queen and princes and princesses. I shouldn't know how to behave."

"Never mind that," said the King. "If you are your ordinary self you will be just right. Please come back with me and help us. The Queen loves our children dearly, but there are so many of them. We cannot take care of them without a nurse. Please, please come. You

shall go home in a year with a suitable reward."

So Clover agreed and held out her hands to the King who grasped them in his cold ones and pulled her down, down, down into the depths of the dark pool.

The royal children gathered round her like bees round a clover flower. She was so gentle that they tried to behave well to please her, and so gay that they never wondered what to do next. She taught them to skip with ropes of water-weed and to weave rushes into mats and little caps. She never forgot to tuck them up and kiss them good night, and she sang them to sleep with a lullaby.

While Clover was living in the kingdom under the

water, the Queen had another baby, a little prince. He was very small and frail and the Queen was so occupied in tending him that the other children were left entirely in Clover's care. The new prince was named Berry as, by this time, the rowan berries were ripe and red. Clover threaded some of the berries on a string and hung them over the baby's cradle. This pleased the Queen as fairy people believe that rowan berries are lucky and act as a charm.

Then the rowan leaves began to turn colour and fall and float on the surface of the pool. The royal children caught them in their silver hands and carried them off to play with. Clover asked the King if she might go back to her own world for just one hour to gather acorns for the children.

"They have never seen an acorn," she said, "and there will be hundreds under the oaks in the wood. They will be happy all the winter playing with them."

"But supposing you never come back!" said the King. "No, stay with us. We love you so."

"I promise to come back," said Clover and all the little princes and princesses said together:

"She never breaks a promise. She will come back."

So Clover was allowed her one hour on dry land, gathering acorns in the basket she had woven of rushes. Once she heard the sound of her father's axe in the distance, but she did not try to find him. She was afraid that he might prevent her from going back to the children.

The royal children were delighted with the acorns. They made toy pipes to smoke and tiny cups and saucepans. Clover showed them how to make acorn men. They had never had dolls to play with and they liked their acorn men so much that they took them to bed with them.

Time flew by and Clover could hardly believe her ears when the King said that a year had passed and it was time for her to go home.

"Don't leave us! Don't leave us!" begged the royal children. "Stay with us for ever!"

But though Clover loved them dearly, she longed to see her father and mother and sisters once more.

"I will come back if you are ever in trouble," she said to the Queen, bending to kiss Prince Berry who was now plump and strong, with green curls all over his head.

The King gave her a heavy purse and in a twinkling she found herself on the shores of the pool. Thin, faint cries came from under the water: "Goodbye, nurse! Goodbye, Clover! Never forget us!"

Clover hurried home and told her story while the family listened.

"Aren't you going to open your purse?" reminded Rose and Snowdrop. Clover opened it and out fell a shower of gold coins, spilling on to her lap and rolling on to the floor.

The money was useful as the woodcutter was a poor man. They all had new boots and new cloaks and hoods for the winter, and the woodcutter bought himself a sharp new axe.

Clover often thought of the Water Folk but her parents did not want her to visit the pool for fear the King might persuade her to go back.

One wintry night, when the snow was on the

ground, there was a tap on the window. As the wood-cutter drew the curtain he saw a strange face outside. Long green hair dripped down, hung with gleaming icicles. There was a crown on the head which shone gold even among the driving snowflakes. It was the King of the pool.

"Come in, Your Majesty," said the woodcutter, opening the door. "Come in and get warm." But one hot breath from the blazing fire made the King feel faint and drove him back into the cold.

"I cannot! I cannot! Please forgive me," he gasped. "It is Clover I want to see."

Clover came forward and stood in the doorway.

"Prince Berry is ill," explained the King. "He won't eat or sleep and the other children are pining too. The Queen can only weep. Please come back if only to tell us what we ought to do."

"Of course I will come, at once," said Clover, putting on her thick snow boots and her warm cloak and hood. "Don't be anxious, father. I shall come home again."

The King struggled along as best he could, unused to dry land or snow and when they reached the pool he drew Clover down through a hole in the ice where the black water showed.

The lovely Queen was weeping as she hushed the wailing baby in her arms and the other children crouched miserably beside her. When they saw who it was they jumped up and down and clapped their silver hands and danced round Clover on their silver feet, their green hair tossing.

Clover took the baby in her arms and rocked him

and sang to him till he fell asleep. Then she brushed and combed the tangled hair of the bigger children, and washed them and put them to bed. Before they went to sleep she told them about the snow in the wood and the huge log fire leaping up the chimney in the cottage. She told them about the snowman that she and her sisters were going to make the next day, and the old hat of her father's they were going to put on his head.

The next morning the Queen begged her to stay, but she shook her head.

"Listen to me," she said to the children. "I will visit you every Sunday and tell you a story and put you to bed. It will be a rest for your mother. Be good children, and I will come."

"But we do not know which day is Sunday," said the children. "All the days are alike to us, living under the water."

"Listen for the church bells," said Clover. "When you hear them ringing you will know that it is Sunday and that I shall be coming to see you."